THE STRENGTH OF GRACE

A. D. Hulstrom

CROSSBOOKS
PUBLISHING

CrossBooks™
A Division of LifeWay
1663 Liberty Drive
Bloomington, IN 47403
www.crossbooks.com
Phone: 1-866-879-0502

First published by CrossBooks 5/16/2012

ISBN: 978-1-4627-1843-6 (sc)
ISBN: 978-1-4627-1844-3 (e)
ISBN: 978-1-4627-1845-0 (hc)

Library of Congress Control Number: 2012908632

Printed in the United States of America
This book is printed on acid-free paper.

PART ONE

The Tragedy

Chapter 1

The pain and anguish were so all-consuming that I almost missed the soft knock on the front door. With my breath held tightly in my chest, I heard the door gently open. When I looked up, I saw Devon coming around the corner into the little bedroom where I sat on the floor.

"I'm so sorry," he said as he fell down onto his knees beside me. "What can I do?"

"Stay with me," I told him, looking into his face; his warm, caring eyes so close to mine. My face was tear-stained, and my eyes were swollen. Within his eyes I could see my own hurt, pain, and despair reflected back at me.

"Absolutely." He put an arm around me, and I leaned my head on his shoulder. I wanted to close my eyes and pretend everything was okay, that my family was intact and nothing so tragic had ever happened. His voice broke over me, washing away the illusion I was trying so hard to build. "Is she okay?" he asked. I nodded and pulled back the blanket from the small bundle on my lap. He drew in his breath quickly as he stared down into the angelic face whose body was held within the circle of my arms, safe and sound. "She is so beautiful."

"And a miracle. The doctor said that it was a miracle she survived at all, let alone with no injuries." Again tears followed the tracks down my face.

"Have you a name for her?" he asked, not able to pull his eyes off her tiny, peaceful face.

"Yes." No sooner had I said it than I broke down into sobs again for the thousandth time in the last two days. He held me close, and just his presence was comforting; so solid beside me. When I was finally in control again, I told him. It was barely a whisper, but somehow he heard. "Grace Elizabeth."

"That's beautiful." He looked down at her and repeated it. "Grace Elizabeth. It fits her." He looked over at me and smiled.

"God's grace saved her, so it seems appropriate for her. Elizabeth after her mother. Oh, Devon, it's not fair! Why them? Why? What hope can her future possibly hold now?" I was shaking with the sobs that racked my body, surprised I had anything left in me with which to cry. He gently took Grace Elizabeth and laid her in the small bassinet. He came back and took me in his arms, closer now without the child in my arms.

"Cry it all out, I'll be here."

"I don't know … if I can make it … through this," I told him between sobs.

"You can, Alyse. I know you can. You're strong, and I'll be right here. You have to pull through for Grace Elizabeth. You are her future, and she needs you."

"I'm not strong enough."

"Yes you are; you'll see. You'll find your strength." He sounded so sure. I desperately wanted to believe him. I needed to believe him. My life had been turned upside down within a matter of hours. And now all I had left was one small baby.

"My family was my strength, and now they're gone. My father, my sister, my brother: gone. She never even got to hold her own child." I thought about my sister, Elizabeth, and how vibrant with life she had been. I thought about the car accident that had taken her life as well as the lives of my father and younger brother. Now I was entrusted with the care of an extension of that life—her child. "I just don't know."

"You've still got Grace; she's your family. And Drew," he added hesitantly. He then quickly added, "Come on, let's let her sleep. Have you had lunch?" He helped me up, and we went quietly to the small kitchen. I headed out to the front porch while Devon made us each a sandwich. It was a beautiful summer day in late June. Once outside with the sunshine and the fresh air, I felt myself begin to relax. Devon came out with the sandwiches, making sure the screen shut quietly behind him. We sat in companionable silence while Devon ate. I didn't have the heart to tell him I wasn't hungry. After glancing over at him, I set my sandwich down on the small table between us. I noticed again how handsome he was, with dark brown hair and vivid blue-green eyes. He was tall, six-foot-two, and well-muscled from an active lifestyle of biking, hiking, and anything else he could do outdoors. Confidence and self-assurance exuded from him, but one could still sense just a hint of his gentle spirit. I glanced up and saw him watching me, a thoughtful expression on his face. He seemed to know what I needed without a word passing between us as he reached out his hand and took mine, and then sat back and closed his eyes.

We sat out on the front porch for a while, the silence a peaceful blanket over the two of us. After a while he started talking, just chatting about whatever came to mind, but Devon was obviously avoiding the subject of family. If he wasn't going to bring it up, neither was I. He paused in the conversation, and I knew what he was thinking. Then, finally, he got up the nerve.

"Does Drew know about this?" he asked, holding tight to my hand. He looked intensely into my eyes, and I had to look away. I would have gotten up to avoid the question, but he was holding my hand tightly, which I guessed was exactly his intent.

"No," I said, but I refused to let the tears fall. Devon already knew this, why would he bring it up? All it did was cause me to remember that night, at my dad's house. "He said he was leaving for good. He and Dad really got into it. It was the same old argument—when was Drew going to do something with his life, and Drew yelling about it being his life and my dad needed to let go and allow him to live it. He told me he'd be in touch as soon as he could, but only if I didn't tell Dad." I could not stop the tears anymore, so I gave up trying, and they fell silently as I thought of my older brother. "He hasn't called yet, and it's been six weeks since he left."

"I'm sure he'll call any day now," Devon told me. He closed his arms around me, and we sat that way until we heard soft crying coming through the monitor. "Sounds like you are needed," he laughed gently. He pulled back my face and looked into my eyes. I slowly got up and went into the house, Devon following behind me.

"Can you make a bottle for me? Everything is sitting on the counter. Just add the small container of formula and shake it up," I said over my shoulder as I continued to the bedroom. I picked up little Grace and held her tightly as I slid back down to the ground. Devon came in just after that, and within seconds, she was quietly eating.

"You really ought to get some more furniture in here," he remarked, looking around my bare guestroom as he sat down on the floor next to me. Taking in the room myself, I knew he was right. All it held was a bassinet and a small table with a lamp.

"I can't bear to go over and get all of it."

"You're going to have to sooner or later," he told me. We sat in silence while Grace finished her bottle. I gently set it down, propped her on my shoulder, and patted her like they'd shown me how to do at the hospital. I was so absorbed with what I was doing that Devon's voice nearly startled me.

"May I hold her?" he asked.

I tried not to show my surprise as I gently turned to face him. "Sure, but you have to hold her head gently. She is only two days old."

"I know. I was five when my brother Ryan was born." Gently, he took Grace Elizabeth from me. "She is so beautiful. She has your family's dark blue eyes," he remarked.

"By the way, how is Ryan?" I asked, steering the subject away from my family, desperate to distract myself.

"He is excited about transferring closer for college this fall."

"Will it be nice to have your little brother around again?" I asked. I knew Ryan was Devon's only family, except for the aunt who had raised them after his parents' plane had gone down in the Mediterranean Sea when Devon was ten.

"Yeah, it will." He looked lost in his own thoughts, so I didn't ask any more questions. I wasn't in the mood to talk about family, anyway.

Little Grace Elizabeth quickly fell asleep again, and after we put her back in her bassinet, we stood around it, looking down at her. "Babies are supposed to be a great joy, but I can't even look at her without thinking of my sister."

"It won't always be like this. You'll have to let her go in your own time, Alyse. But it will hurt for a long time." His voice took on a husky tone, and I could tell he was lost in his thoughts while he spoke, remembering.

"I know. I remember when I lost my mother to cancer when I was only eight. But this is different. Elizabeth and Gavin were so young, only eighteen and sixteen. And my dad, still with so much life left in him. It hurts, Devon. It hurts so much." I was sobbing again. I had given up trying to stop myself. This was the first time I had said my thoughts out loud regarding the accident, and it felt good to let it out. I cried awhile longer, and then just stood in the silence of Grace's room, Devon's presence so strong beside me and peace of a sleeping baby filling my senses. Quietly, so as not to wake her, Devon and I left the room.

"Shall I make us some dinner?" I asked Devon.

"Why don't we just order a pizza and eat on the front porch," Devon said, smiling.

"Alright," I said, smiling despite myself. "But I don't understand your obsession with my front porch." He just smiled.

"When you live in an apartment as long as I have, you learn to appreciate some odd things, such as a front porch."

We ate and talked and laughed. His presence was soothing, his voice like a balm. And for awhile I was able to forget about my grief, that is, until Grace Elizabeth let out a healthy cry. I longed for the day when the pain would be past and I would only see the child and not the ghost of her mother; when I would be able to feel only love and not the pain of loss.

"The busy life of a Mommy," Devon said, smiling at me. He got up and followed me into the guest bedroom. "What is little Grace going to call you?" Devon asked, looking serious as I picked her up and turned to him.

"I don't know. I haven't really thought about it."

"She could call you 'mom'-"

"Oh, I don't know about that. I'm not her mother."

"Aunt Alyse," he said, trying it out. He came up to me and carefully put his arms around us. "I like the sound of Mommy better, and I think you do too, Alyse." He looked down into my eyes, kissed and released me. "Well, I'd better get going." He turned to leave the room.

"No, Devon! Wait," I said, starting after him. "This is my first night alone with her, and I'm scared. Will you please stay? Just stay here in the house with me … with her."

"Of course, I'll stay with you. All you ever have to do is ask." He turned and I followed him into the living room. We sat down on the floor and Devon turned on the TV.

We sat there for awhile, watching TV together. Grace fell asleep in my arms, and I fell asleep in Devon's. Grace woke me up several times throughout the night. She only woke Devon up the first time, and after that I put her in her bassinet and stayed with her in the guestroom. I slept better just knowing someone else was there with me. The next morning, I made Devon breakfast, even though I was dead tired.

"I'll try to come over as early as I can, but I'll have to do some overtime to get some things done this week, make up time for missing yesterday," he told me.

"I'm sorry," I told him, a sense of guilt creeping over me for having made him miss work on account of me.

"No," he said gently. "I wanted to be here. I'm glad you called."

"Really?"

"Really," he replied. "My boss let me off without a problem. He said he understood; that he had three kids of his own."

"What did you tell him?" I asked suspiciously.

"That my girlfriend just came home from the hospital with a baby," he said, grinning, seemingly quite proud of himself.

"Devon!"

"I know," he said, still grinning. "He congratulated me and said he wished he would have known sooner and then he could have bought some kind of gift."

"Devon Casey, I can't believe you!" I couldn't help laughing, though. And it felt so good. We were still laughing as he left for his job as an architect in a successful company downtown. After only one year on the job he was already working his way up. He knew almost everyone. His personality, outgoing, fun-loving, and easy to be around and talk to, allowed him such mobility and success. I was so proud of him and felt such gratitude for his attention to me.

After a morning nap and some lunch, I had finally worked up the nerve to go to my father's house to get some of Grace Elizabeth's things, when the doorbell rang. I had no clue as to who it could be. I went up to the door and looked through the window.

"Drew!" I yelled and throw open the door. "Oh, I missed you so much," I cried, throwing my arms around my brother.

"Hey there, little sister," he said, returning my embrace.

"I am only 16 minutes younger," I retorted. All my life he had been calling me 'little sister,' though people often guessed we were twins. Drew and I both had our family's dark golden blonde hair and clear blue-green eyes, we were both slim and tall, though in high school he shot past me to just over 6 feet. Thankfully, that was where the similarities ended, Drew was all man and very much a flirt; whereas I was happy to be in the background whenever possible.

"That makes me 16 minutes older than you, making you my little sister." He laughed. I really didn't mind it anymore. Now it was more like an old joke we shared, and that was something I needed now more than ever. He and Grace Elizabeth were the only family I had left now. Andrew must have noticed my change of moods.

"You okay? You don't look so happy to see me anymore."

"Of course I'm happy to see you. You are my brother, and you are always welcome wherever I am."

"Thank you, Alyse." He followed me inside and set his things down by the door. "So, what's going on? Why the long face?"

"So, what are you doing here?" I asked, trying to sound casual, like I wasn't trying to change the subject to delay the inevitable. I didn't want to tell him about the accident just yet. Iwanted to keep the good feeling of being with my brother alive for just a few more minutes before the grief set back in. I knew telling him of it would force me to relive it, something I did anyway, every time my thoughts drifted off.

"Well, I said I'd get in touch soon, so here I am."

"You look awful," I said, noting his clothes, face, and hair.

"Thanks, Alyse," he said sarcastically. "After I left, I went as far as I could. But I soon ran out of money, so I had to do some odd jobs and hitchhike back." He looked proud of himself.

"Drew, that's so dangerous. Why didn't you call me?" I was worried about him. He was 22, and had no job, not many friends, and no place he could call his own. All he had he could carry around with him, except for a few things he had left with me.

"I wanted to surprise you." He was so laid back.

"Well, you did."

"Are you mad?" For a moment, he looked worried.

"No. No, of course not."

"Good. So," he started, making himself comfortable, "how's the fam?"

"Well, Drew, a lot has happened since you left." I just couldn't bring myself to say it. Thank goodness I didn't have to go on, Grace Elizabeth woke up and demanded my attention. I started to get up when Andrew stopped me.

"What's that?"

"It's a baby," I replied, walking toward her bedroom.

"I realize its a baby, Alyse. Is it Elizabeth's baby?" It was a simple question, but it struck a painful chord. All I could do was nod as he got up to follow me. I knelt down and picked up the crying baby, then turned to Drew.

"She's so beautiful," he said softly. I didn't even ask, I just handed her over to her uncle. He took her gently and I helped him position her properly. Still staring at her angelic little face, he sank down onto the floor, totally wrapped up in his niece. Finally, he remembered me. "So, where is Lizzy? Are you babysitting?"

I dropped down onto the floor next to him. One look into my face was all he needed. He looked again at his little niece, and tears slowly fell onto the blanket wrapped around her little body. I had only seen him cry once before, when we were eight, and our mother had finally been released from her battle with cancer. My big strong brother hadn't cried since. Finally, I heard his voice. "What happened?"

"Well, it was a car accident. She was in the back seat. Dad was driving, and they think he might not have been watching, and – and … Oh, Drew, they are all gone!" I couldn't say anymore. The tears spilled down my cheeks. "I –"

"NO!" he yelled. He handed the startled baby to me and jumped up off the floor. Then he stormed out of the house and ran down the street. I followed him to the door and then just watched him go. The helplessness I felt was overwhelming as the innocent baby in my arms cried out her own discomfort.

He came back three hours later. Grace Elizabeth was asleep again. Saying nothing to me, he went and stood by her bassinet for a long time. I let him grieve on his own.

After awhile, he came into the kitchen and sat down hard at the table, dropping his head into his hands. His voice raw and rough with his grief, he asked me, "What is her name?"

"Grace Elizabeth Sheridon."

"That's beautiful. Did you name her?"

"Yes. I think it fits her perfectly."

"I think so, too, Alyse. You did a good job." Drew raised his head and looked up at me, his eyes full of pain. "Tell me the rest."

"Drew, I-"

"Tell me!" he said so forcefully that he startled me. He hadn't talked to me like that since grade school. We had always been so close. I turned away from him and when I turned back, he had his hands over his eyes and his voice sounded muffled. "I'm sorry, Aly. It just hurts so much."

"I know it does. I'm hurting, too." I sat down next to him. "Dad and Gavin died instantly. They were going pretty fast. Elizabeth wasn't wearing a seatbelt, and lost too much blood. They – they couldn't save her, but they saved her baby. The doctors said it was a miracle she survived. That is what made me think of the name Grace."

"When did this happen?"

"Three days ago. The funeral is tomorrow."

"Looks like I came back just in time," he said grimly, staring off out the window, lost in his own thoughts. We were sitting there in silence when I heard a car pull up out front.

"Hi, Honey, I'm home," I heard Devon call from the living room.

"In the kitchen," I called back.

"Hello – hey, Drew. It's good to see you."

"Hi, Devon." The two men shook hands and then Devon sat down with us at the table. Of course, Grace Elizabeth picked this moment to wake up. I quickly made a bottle and headed off, leaving the two men on their own. After feeding her and cuddling just a bit, I brought her in to the kitchen with me. Handing her off to Devon, I turned toward the refrigerator to get dinner started.

It was a pleasant evening. We sat outside for awhile and talked of a simpler time, our childhood. Little Grace Elizabeth had revived in us a feeling of youth, even amidst the tragedy and all despair we felt. It was wonderful to be able to relive these memories, and at the same time it was painful. Drew and I had shared a lot of hard times, but we'd always been there for each other, and I hoped our lives would continue that way.

"So, Aly, are you keeping her?" Drew asked me.

"Yes, I would really like to. You know that you and I are her only living relatives. In the will, Dad left everything to me." There I stopped.

"He would do that," Drew retorted.

"He was mad. I believe that he would have changed it back, Drew, if he'd had more time."

"I know." All was silent for a moment. "Then you own this house now."

"Yes, no more rent, just mortgage payments."

"So, Grace is yours."

"Yes, temporary custody for now, I'm sure they'll grant me permanent custody."

"Just making sure." He turned and looked out the kitchen window, not really seeing the scene outside. His eyes unfocused, he looked like he was debating his options.

"You know that you are more than welcome to stay and help me. I start work in September."

"I'll think about it." Drew took a deep breath and finally looked a bit more relaxed. "So, they finally let you out of college. I'm sorry I missed graduation."

"It's alright."

"You found a job around here?"

"Yes, teaching third grade at Southside Elementary."

"Good, good. Well, I'm going to shower, then hit the hay. I'm dead tired." We all cringed at that. "Sorry, that was unintended," he said quietly as he left the room.

I nodded. After Drew went inside, Grace Elizabeth woke up again. I went in and brought her out to Devon. "Would you mind feeding her?"

"Sure," he said, gently taking her from me. "You look really tired, Alyse. Why don't you go on to bed. I'll put Grace to bed when she's done, then leave."

"Thanks, Devon. Between her and my brother, I haven't gotten much sleep." I started to relax when I finally caught all he had said. "Devon, "I said, turning to him. He was so good with Grace Elizabeth, his confidence gave me confidence. "I would like it if you would stay with me again, like last night." I got up and sat down next to him and leaned over onto him. "I could use your strength." He smiled and nodded.

That night, I must have been more exhausted than I realized. I woke up in my bed, and didn't remember how I gotten there. I quickly got up and went into the kitchen.

"Good morning, sleepyhead," Devon said. "Your brother makes a pretty good breakfast."

I smiled. The table was loaded with eggs, toast, bacon, and pancakes. "Where is he?"

"He's in the living room with Grace," replied Devon, piling his plate with more food. When I walked in, I was a little surprised. He was asleep on the couch, and next to him was Grace Elizabeth's bassinet. I walked over to the bassinet and peeked in. She was awake, and she looked up at me with her big beautiful eyes.

"Good morning, Sweetie," I said softly. I picked her up and carried her over to the window. The morning rays from the sun were just cutting through the midnight mist. "A beautiful new day is dawning, Grace Elizabeth Sheridon." I held her close to me. Drew came up and stood beside me.

"A beautiful day is dawning," he said softly.

I nodded. I heard Devon's footsteps coming from the kitchen.

"Well, Mom," said Devon, putting his hand on my shoulder. "I'll be here whenever you need me."

"Me, too," said Drew.

"I'm very thankful for that." I turned and looked back out the window. "You guys are my only family now." Both presences felt very strong to me. They both emanated with the strength I thought I lacked. They were my rock, and together, I thought we could make it through anything. "Well, today I'll need both of you. Today is the funeral." Devon took my hand, and Drew put his hand upon my shoulder. We stood for a few minutes in silence. Then each headed his own way to prepare for the somber day that lay ahead.

Chapter 2

"Hurry up! We have to be at the church before one," I called out to Drew.

"Be there in a minute!" he called back.

"You said that five minutes ago," I reminded him.

"I mean it this time."

"Are you sure you want to take Grace? I mean – do you really think it's a good idea?" Devon asked.

"Yes," I told him, not allowing my voice to carry the doubt I felt inside.

Devon nodded, then walked to the car with all of Grace Elizabeth's things. I watched him go, then looked down at my niece.

"He's a good guy, Sweetie. We're lucky to have him around."

"Well, thank you."

I whirled around to see that Drew had finally emerged from the bathroom. "You, too, Drew," I said, smiling at my brother.

"You mean Devon?" he asked.

"Yeah, but I appreciate your help as well."

"Thanks." He walked over to the couch and picked up his wallet. "Ready?"

"Yes, let's go."

"You know," Drew started, as he walked with me toward the door, "it's obvious he's loves you."

"What makes you say that?" I asked him, feeling my heart beat faster.

"I can tell by the way he looks at you, by the way he talks to you, the way he acts when you're around. You know, the little things."

I thought about what Drew had said during the car ride to the funeral. Did I love Devon? I thought I did, but how could I know for sure? Little did I know at the time that I would soon have to find the answer to that very question.

I wished with all my heart that I could have been anywhere but at a funeral for my father, sister and brother. I cried the whole time. My head hurt; my heart hurt. Little Grace Elizabeth slept almost the whole time. And when she woke up, she didn't cry. It was almost as if she knew I needed her peacefulness.

After my father, sister, and brother were laid to rest in the little cemetery where my mother was buried, I felt that a very large piece of me had been buried with them, and I was sure there was no way to get it back. Why had Dad turned his attention from the road? Why had Elizabeth taken off her seatbelt? Why had Grace Elizabeth been spared? "Why" questions floated in and out of my mind, driving me crazy, chasing my sanity around and around until I felt for sure I would lose it for good.

After the dirt had been filled in over my family, my life, we headed back into the church. My soul ached, it was all too painful, more than I could handle. And, though I didn't want to admit it to myself, I had my doubts that God was with me. I was ashamed of these thoughts, but they didn't stop. Like a broken record, they chased my faith through my consciousness, trying to drag it down into the bottomless pit of despair where my heart had been not all that long ago. He could have saved them, why didn't He? And so on until I was sure I would go mad. Then I thought about little Grace Elizabeth. Had God saved her? The doctors had said she shouldn't have made it. Why had she? Only in looking back can I see the answer. But at that moment, all I could feel was pain and doubt. All these thoughts ran crazy through my mind as I sat there, the reception going on all around me. Finally, I couldn't take it anymore.

I handed Grace Elizabeth to Devon, who was standing beside me. As I ran out of the church, I could feel the fresh tears stinging my eyes. I could hear Devon start to move behind me. Drew must have grabbed his arm to stop him as I burst out into the parking lot, alone at last.

I didn't stop running until I got to the graves. I fell down on my knees next to my father's. As I closed my eyes, I could almost feel his strong arms around me.

"No!" I screamed. "It's not fair!" I beat the ground with my fists as I cried out, and soon all my energy and some of my anger had dissipated. I sat down and leaned against the tombstone, feeling spent and empty. Next to my father's grave was my mother's. As I turned to look at it, memories came flooding back, all those times my father and I had put flowers on the grave, all the times he had comforted me after she had passed away. Then I let my mind go even further back. She'd been battling with the cancer for about a year before she died. That had been a very hard year for all of us. She had been diagnosed just after my brother, Gavin, had been born. It had been such a bittersweet event, but then, my life seemed to be full of such moments.

Now Elizabeth and Gavin were gone as well. The pain cut deep, the wound still fresh. I went to Gavin's grave. "Don't worry, little brother, I'll never forget you." I sat down next to the tombstone and talked to him for awhile. After that, a certain peace settled over me.

I turned toward Elizabeth's grave. As I looked at her grave, my mind kept a picture of Grace Elizabeth ever in the forefront. I thought about my little sister and, without meaning to, my mind wandered back to the night that had caused Grace Elizabeth's appearance. It was getting to be very late, and my father, Drew, and I were waiting for Elizabeth to return. It was one of the few weekends that we all spent together. I remember looking over at my father and seeing the worried expression on his face …

"She should have been home over an hour ago!" he exclaimed. I tried hard to keep my face straight. Dad always worried far too much.

"I'm sure she is fine. She is a responsible girl." I tried my best to calm him. The truth was that I was starting to get a little nervous myself.

We sat in silence for a few minutes before the phone rang. All three of us leaped for it, but my brother and I backed off after a look from my father.

By the look on his face, I could tell that whatever he was hearing wasn't good news. I felt myself start to shiver, and then felt Drew's hand on my shoulder. Slowly, Dad hung up the phone. He went to the closet and got his coat, then turned back toward us.

"Alyse, stay here with Gavin. Drew, come with me."

"No," I said, standing up. "I want to go, I know it's about Liz."

"Alyse, I need you to stay-"

"I'll stay with Gavin. Alyse can go in my place." I looked thankfully at my brother. He smiled and then gave me a quick hug.

We headed out to the car. Dad told me what had happened on the way to the hospital. "I knew I shouldn't have let her out of the house with that boy. He – they – she called the police after he let her go, but …" He couldn't go on, there were tears in his eyes. I felt silent tears fall down my own cheeks and reached out to take my father's hand …

I clearly remember walking into the hospital room and seeing my little sister. She was badly beaten and hooked up to machines. She wasn't awake. They quickly ushered us out into the waiting room. They never found the boy again. He stole some money and the car from his parents. They found the car, but what happened to him, no one knows.

I can still clearly remember that night. I looked over at my sister's grave. "You were so brave, Lizzy. I don't think I could have made it."

"You know, she counted on your strength to help her through that. She always knew she could lean on you for support."

I heard his voice but didn't have the energy to turn toward my brother. "How did you know what I was talking about?"

Kneeling down next the tombstone, Drew peered into my face. "I can read your mind, little sister. Don't forget, we're linked." He touched his hand to his temple then to his heart, and winked at me, then he took my hand and looked into my eyes. "Are you going to be alright?"

I nodded. We sat in silence for a few minutes. I knew he had something to say, but I also knew he knew I needed this silence, even just for a few short minutes.

Finally, Drew sighed. "There are people inside who are asking where you are, Aly," he said softly. "Why don't you come on inside." Though it was against everything thought and feeling within me, I let my brother help me up and tow me back inside the building.

"Good-bye," I whispered into the wind.

Part Two

The Choice

CHAPTER 3

"She won't stop crying, and I don't know what's wrong with her," Drew said as soon as I walked in the door.

"Have you tried changing her?" I asked as I set my briefcase and school work down by the door.

"Of course, I'm not an idiot!! I've been dealing with her for the last four months," he yelled at me. I tried not to shrink back as I took Grace and went into our bedroom, deliberately shutting the door behind me. I held my small niece close to me and paced the room. Within minutes she was quiet. She stared up at me and I could no longer hold back the tears. They flowed unchecked down my cheeks. My brother had truly hurt me this afternoon, and it wasn't the first time. It was happening more and more often. Rude, implying comments, expressions that made it easy to read into his mind, things said under his breath; such were part of the game for him. They had been never directed straight at me, though, not before the Accident.

I continued to pace with little Grace, and after awhile, she fell asleep. Gently, I put her down in her crib and watched her for a few moments. She looked so peaceful and content. Watching her, it was hard to believe everything wasn't right with the world.

Quietly, so as not to wake her, I changed and thought back through the past four months. My brother and I had gone through our father's house, and though it had been hard, we'd sold it. I had cried myself to sleep that night. My father had owned two small rental houses. Their mortgages were smaller; I lived in one, and we could use the extra income from the other, so we decided to keep them.

When I'd started my job, Drew had stayed home to take care of Grace. Though I didn't know much about babies, Grace was a sweetheart with a easygoing temperament that made her enjoyable to be around. Drew was very good with her, but every once in awhile she'd get into crying fits, and wouldn't stop unless I walked her around. The little baby had accepted me as her mother and it touched my heart deeply.

I loved my job, and lately I had found myself wishing every once in awhile that I didn't have to come home. This left me feeling horrible, of course, for I loved Grace and Drew, but the stress was becoming too much. I guess I'd never realized how much work a baby could be. But, through it all,I never once regretted my decision to keep her.

Once I got home, Drew left to work the evening shift at a nearby factory. He'd just started his job two weeks earlier, and I was under the impression that he was glad to get away.

I left my room and headed toward the front door, where I had left my briefcase. I carried it to the dining room table and spread out its contents. As I started going through papers, I realized that I was glad it was Friday, meaning I would be spending the next day with Devon.

As I thought about Devon, I smiled for the first time since I had walked in the door two hours earlier. I graded papers and organized my lessons and thought about Devon long into the early evening, until Grace woke up. We hung out together and just relaxed.

I was so relaxed, I fell asleep. I had meant to stay awake until Drew got home, we needed to talk. However, when I woke up, it was early morning, and he was already gone again. I tried not to let it get me down.

Devon came over around eleven, and we took Grace with us out to lunch. As we ate, I noticed he seemed preoccupied with something, but I had enough on my plate, so I let it go and just enjoyed my lunch. When we got back to the house, I put Grace down for a nap. When I came back into the living room, Devon was standing in exactly the same place.

"What's wrong?" I asked him. He just shook his head and attempted a smile. It didn't work. I took his hand and led him over to the couch, ignoring the growing sense of dread building up in my gut. "You know you can talk to me about anything."

He nodded and pulled me up against him. I held onto him tight and tried not to cry. Nothing was ever going to be the same if he told me what was wrong, I just knew it. I suspected suffering in every aspect of my life now, like I was just waiting for each piece to fall. The new me didn't expect anything to go right, and when something did I was suspicious.

"Alyse, I need to talk to you," he said as he pulled away and looked into my eyes.

'Here it comes,' I thought, and braced myself for the worst. I looked down at my hands. He didn't say anything, so I finally looked up at him. He was staring at me with such intensity that it scared me. "What, Devon?" Had that been my voice? It had sounded like it had come from so far away.

"Alyse," he started, and let go of one of my hands. He slid off the couch and opened a small box. "Will you marry me?"

I didn't know what to say. I was totally speechless. I knew I loved Devon, so why wouldn't my mouth say yes?

"Before you answer," Devon continued, taking both my hands once more, "I want to say that I love you with all my heart, mind, and soul. I always will."

Still, my mouth would not work. I wanted to shout that I loved him, too. That, yes, I would marry him, but it just wouldn't come out.

"There's something else," Devon said before I could manage to respond. I looked at him, and he looked troubled. "My company is transferring me."

My whole body went numb. I couldn't even look up at him. It was either marry him now, or lose him forever. Suddenly, my heart hurt and I felt like I couldn't breathe.

"Alyse?" Devon tightened his grip on my hand and tilted my face up with his other hand.

"When?" Finally, I had found my voice.

"Right after Christmas."

I only nodded and looked back down at my hands. Slowly, my mind began to work. I knew I loved Devon, but did I love him enough to leave my hometown, my brother, and my job? It seemed silly, but I felt closer to my dad, Elizabeth, and Gavin here. Could I really leave all of that for love? Was it that strong? I just wasn't sure.

"Where?"

"Seattle, Washington. It is a better opportunity for me. I want you to come with me, you and Grace."

To me, that seemed like a long way from my suburb of Chicago, and even further from my brother.

"Just take your time, Alyse. I can wait for you." He leaned back on the couch and pulled me over to him. I leaned against him and cried. It seemed that was all I ever did lately.

After awhile, I had no more tears. Pulling away from Devon, I looked into his face. He tried to smile, but I could tell that he was hurting, too.

He rose up from the couch and started a fire in the fireplace. He went into the kitchen and came back a few minutes later with two mugs of hot chocolate. It wasn't until then that I realized how cold I was. He sat down and handed me a mug. I curled up next to him, and stared into the fire. So unsure of myself was I that I didn't even trust myself enough to talk. I just sat there in a ball at Devon's side and stared into the fire.

That night, as I lay in bed, I found that I had no more tears. I couldn't cry at all; not for my broken relationship with my brother, not for my decision concerning Devon, not even for my lost family. I found that my whole body was numb.

All through the next week, I thought about what I should do. I wasn't sure my heart was ready for total commitment and a huge move, but I didn't want to lose Devon. I prayed continually that God would give me the wisdom and the strength to do what was right.

Finally, by the end of the week, I thought I knew what I wanted to do. Devon never pushed me to make up my mind, but I could tell that he was getting very anxious.

Saturday, I felt confident enough to know what to do. Devon came over and, as usual, we took Grace with us out to lunch. When we got back, I put Grace down for her nap, and Devon and I sat on the porch with hot chocolate and watched the tiny snowflakes fall. It was so beautiful. Devon was patient, but after awhile, he turned to me and I knew what he wanted. Slowly, I turned to face him. I saw the questioning look in his eyes.

"Devon, I think I have an answer for you," I said.

"Alyse, I want you to be sure," he replied.

I nodded. Gently, I took his hand in mine. "Devon, I would love to be your wife."

He sat there a moment, until my words finally sank in. He jumped up and pulled me up with him. He swung me around in his arms. "Oh, Alyse. I love you so much!" he kept repeating over and over. Each time he said it, a little piece of my confidence chipped away, like a chisel chipping away at a block of ice. For the first time since I had made my decision, I doubted myself.

For the remaining weeks until Thanksgiving, Devon continued to be the happiest man alive, and I continued to doubt myself. Maybe it was because I had no one else to talk to; Drew avoided me most of the time; Elizabeth was gone, so was Dad. I couldn't talk to Devon, and Grace didn't talk back, although she listened very well. I tried to lay my burden down, but I just couldn't, or wouldn't, let go. For me, life became simply going through the motions, as I felt dead inside.

Thanksgiving came and went. It was a little awkward for me. Between Drew and Devon, I always felt as if I was avoiding something, and I guess I was. The only bright spot was Devon's brother, Ryan. He made us all laugh with his goofy jokes and his fun sense of humor. Although I knew he didn't know the details of what was going on inside each of us, I think he could sense that we needed the laughter.

I gave my notice at school. They said they were sad to see me go, but wished me good luck. If only luck was all I needed.

People at the church I had gone to for as long as I could remember all congratulated Devon and me, never realizing the struggle that was going on beneath the surface.

I lay awake many nights rethinking things. Then, finally, about two weeks before Christmas, I cried. With a tremendous thunderstorm, the torrents were loosed, I had finally found my tears once again. I cried throughout most of the night. And when I was finally finished, I knew what I had to do. It was with a heavy heart that I got up the next morning.

That night, we hired a babysitter and went out. When we got back, Devon started a fire. This was our typical Saturday evening of late, to sit around the fire and talk. Tonight, as Devon began to talk excitedly about our future, I just sat back and watched him. As I reached deep down inside me, I felt another part of me dying, but I knew what I had to do. I wondered how much of me would be left after this.

"Alyse, are you okay?" he asked.

"Yes," I managed to say in a fairly normal tone.

"You look a little distant," he replied, and a look of worry flashed across his face.

"I'm sorry. Go on, you were saying something about Ryan." I tried to smile, but I could tell by the look on his face that I was not successful. *My friend*, I thought to myself, *I want to spare you this pain as long as I can.* I felt the hot tears burning behind my eyes, but somehow managed to hold them back.

I listened as he told me that his brother was going to spend Christmas with us. I listened as he related the details of our future as we had planned them out, and I knew I could play this charade no longer. The tears that I had been holding back broke through and fell silently down my cheeks.

Devon turned toward me and stopped in mid sentence. "What is it, darling?" he asked. I couldn't answer, so he swept me up in his strong arms. That only made what I had to do that much harder. I tried to push away, but found that I hadn't the strength. Devon held me tight and murmured softly into my hair, and I knew my heart had just broken again. I felt sure that it would just stop, it was damaged too badly.

I finally pulled away from him. When I looked up, there were tears in his eyes too. "Oh, Devon," I whispered, as I gently took his hand in mine. He didn't look down, but kept his eyes on mine. I think he knew, but it never showed in his eyes. All I saw was unending, unconditional love. As I placed the ring in his hand, the last of my emotion drained out of my body, leaving me numb.

We sat that way for a long time, his hand locked around mine, the ring in the middle. I don't know how long we sat there, it could have been minutes, it could have been years. It didn't really matter.

Gently, he slipped his hand out of mine and looked down at the ring in his hand. He stared at it a moment, then looked back up at me. "Why?"

"Devon, please." It was barely a whisper. I had to look away, and I found myself staring at the place the ring should have been.

"Alyse, I kneed to know."

I felt the full impact of his words, but couldn't look up. "I need to find myself first … too much has happened, it has just taken too much of me. I don't have enough to give you. I'm not a whole person. You deserve someone who can lay her heart at your feet, Devon. I can't do that now. You deserve so much more." I'm not sure just where those words came from, but I knew that was how I felt; everything summed up in a few short sentences, if that was possible.

It was all true; I had nothing left to give. I didn't feel that he should settle for me. I had taken the decision upon myself. It wasn't a question of love, I did love him. Because of that love, I wanted so much more for him. Had he asked me six months ago, maybe things would have been different. It wasn't that I didn't want to marry him, it was just that I needed my own time to heal and put my broken self back together. I had to find myself, finally realizing that no one else could do it for me, and no amount of running or hiding would help me. I had to find a way to rely upon my own strength, however much of it was left.

It felt like it took all that remaining strength, but I started to stand up. Devon reached out and put a hand on my arm. It felt like it was burning into my flesh like hot iron, and I bit back a scream.

"Don't go," Devon said, his voice choked with emotion.

"Devon, no." I started to pull away, but his grip became tighter. He looked up at me, and his eyes were full of pain. Wave upon wave of guilt and anguish washed over me. It was becoming harder to breath. I knew I had to pull away before I was pulled under.

With all the strength left inside my tired body, I managed to free my arm. I took off for my room, not daring to turn around. Once there, I collapsed on the floor. Sobs of agony racked my body. What was I doing? Why was I putting us through this torture? I could go back out there and put a stop to it all, and take back Devon's ring. But I knew that would only hold it at bay for awhile. Soon, even that would wear down, leaving myself raw to the salt grinding into me, to the pain and grief with which I had yet to deal. It was a barrier that just wouldn't hold. I had to let it do its damage so that I could heal properly. There was no putting a band-aid on and forgetting about this one.

I don't know how long I sat on the floor in Grace's room, or even what I was thinking all that time. I probably could have sat there in that trance forever, but little Grace called me back to reality. Gently, I picked her up and started pacing the room. She just kept staring up at me, and her eyes seemed to be saying, "I love you, no matter what."

And finally, my heart began to beat once more.

Part Three

The Heart

CHAPTER 4

"Can you believe it?" he said to his companion. "I can still remember the day her daddy bought that house."

His companion grinned and looked across the street. Clearly, he could see the moving truck and the working men loading it. "It doesn't seem that long ago that she herself moved in."

"And what about that little doll of hers," replied the first man, nodding his head at the scene across the street. A young woman had just come out of the house holding the hand of a small child. She raised her other hand to shade her eyes from the bright July sunshine. The young woman moved with an air of confidence. She stood tall and proud as she surveyed the surrounding scene. She saw the two older men across the street, waved, and started over, still holding the hand of small girl.

"Mommy, where are we going?" she asked me as we walked across the street.

"We are going to say good-bye to Mr. Collins and Mr. Smythe. See them over there on Mr. Collins' porch?" I asked, pointing toward the two older gentlemen.

"Yes, I do. Mommy, I do see them!" She got excited and let go of my hand to hop up the steps to greet our elder neighbors.

"Hello there, Little Grace," Mr. Collins greeted the young girl and flashed a quick smile at me.

"I'm not little," she replied, scrunching up her face. "I just turned four!" She held up four fingers for them to see.

"Oh, my, you certainly are a big girl." The older man smiled and reached out to pull her up into his lap.

"We are going away," she told him, her eyes sparkling with exhilaration.

"Are you excited?" asked another voice. Grace whirled around on Mr. Collins' lap to see Mrs. Collins behind him. She leaped off and threw her arms around the lady who had been like a grandmother to her and a miracle from God to me. "Why don't you come on inside, child. I've got something for you. And you, too, Alyse." She turned and motioned for us to follow her inside.

Mrs. Collins had been watching Grace for the past two and a half years during the school day. She absolutely adored my niece, and had been a great help to me after my brother left. Grace just loved her. She went to the same church, and we had talked long and often the first years after the Accident, after Devon had left. She had helped me rely on my faith and begin to see past the anger I felt and toward the healing that needed to happen.

"Okay, now you have to close your eyes," Mrs. Collins told Grace.

She nodded and closed her eyes. Mrs. Collins went to a cupboard and pulled out a fluffy stuffed bear and placed it in Grace's arms. Grace sucked in her breath and shrieked. She hugged the bear close to her and turned toward me. Her smile made my heart soar.

"What do you say, Grace?" I reminded her.

"Oh, thank you, Mrs. Collins," she replied, throwing her arms around the older woman. Mrs. Collins knelt down and took Grace into her arms. I could see tears slide down her cheeks, and I turned to look out the window at the warm July sky. "Look what I got, Mommy," Grace said, tugging at my hand.

I turned back toward my small niece. Her face was aglow with child-like happiness. I knelt down and swung her up into my arms. I held her close and turned back to Mrs. Collins.

"Alyse, this is for you. Don't lose heart, Dear." She pressed a small devotional into my hands. I looked back up at her, a smile on my face.

"Thank you, thank you so much, for everything."

She smiled and nodded. "These are for you, too," she said, holding out a tin. I took it with my free hand and put my arm around the older woman in an awkward hug.

"What's in it?" Grace asked.

"Homemade cookies for my little sweet," she replied, taking hold of Grace's hand and giving it a quick squeeze. We all turned and headed out onto the porch. I set Grace down and she ran over to show the two elder gentlemen her stuffed bear.

"Is your brother moving with you?" Mrs. Collins asked.

I shook my head and looked across the street. "He's got an apartment in the city with some girl he's seeing. I feel that I've lost him." I continued to stare at the house, afraid to take my eyes off it. "He's the only family I have, besides Grace," I said, talking more to myself.

The older woman reached out and took hold of my hand. I turned and she had tears in her eyes. "If you ever need someone, we're here, always," she replied. "God places people in your life for a reason, Alyse, never forget that." Then, after giving me a quick hug, she went back into the house.

"Come on, Grace. It's time to go." I took hold of her hand, we said our good-byes, and started across the street. "Why don't we go get some lunch, then see if Uncle Drew is home?"

"Yeah!" she replied and started skipping up the steps of our house. I followed her inside to grab my purse and keys.

"What's your bear's name?" I heard one of the moving men ask Grace.

She pushed her lips together and paused before answering, "Elizabeth."

"That's a pretty name," he replied.

"Let's go," I called, so as not to give myself enough time to reflect upon her answer.

"Okay, Mommy," she said, slipping her hand into mine. I smiled down at her and headed toward the door.

"I don't think there is anyone home, Mommy," Grace said, tugging at my hand. She kept looking curiously around the dingy hallway that led to my brother's apartment door.

"Maybe you're right," I replied and started to turn away from the door, just as it started to open.

"Hello." A young woman with cold eyes and a sneer on her face had opened the door just enough to stick her head out of it. "May I help you?"

"Is Andrew Sheridon here?" I asked.

"Depends on who's asking," she said quite nastily, looking from me down to little Grace.

"I'm-"

"Look, I don't really care who you are. Drew isn't here right now, and even if he was, the kid ain't his, so he ain't going to help you. Beat it."

I was so shocked that I just stood there with my mouth hanging open. The woman didn't move, but was obviously waiting for me to leave. All of a sudden, she stood up straighter and smiled, but not at me, at something behind me. I turned to find my brother.

"Hi, Alyse. I see you've met Mandy." He obviously hadn't heard what 'Mandy' had just said to me. "Hi, Little Grace." He knelt down and gave her a quick hug. Then he passed us and gave Mandy a hug and a kiss. Then he remembered us again. "Oh, yeah. Come on in."

"But, Drew-" Mandy started.

"It's okay, Mandy. This is my sister Alyse, and my niece Grace." At least Mandy had the decency to blush a bright red. She turned and apologized, then quickly left the room. "So, what brings you to my neck of the woods?"

"We're leaving this afternoon, Drew. I just thought that we'd come over."

"Is that all?" Drew asked.

"Well, there is still time, if you wanted to-"

"No."

"Drew, if you would just listen-"

"No, Alyse. I'm staying right here in Chicago. I don't want to move to Indianapolis with you."

"I'm going to miss you so much, Drew," I said, trying so hard to hold back the tears.

"I'll miss you, too, Uncle Drew," Grace said, burying herself further back against me.

Drew looked down at Grace. He came over and knelt down beside us. Smiling at Grace, he reached over and touched her bear. "What's this little fellow's name?"

"Elizabeth," she replied.

"Why did you name her that?" he asked. He looked up at me, and for the moment our eyes met, we both relived old memories.

"It's my other name, and it is you and Mommy's sister's name, you know, the one who isn't here anymore."

"Yeah, I know," Drew whispered. "Mandy, come here please." Reluctantly, the woman stuck her head out of a door and looked at Drew. "Will you please take Grace and get her an ice cream cone downstairs." Grace jumped up and danced around while Mandy took the money Drew offered. As soon as they left, tears flooded my eyes.

"Are you going to be okay?" Drew asked me as I followed him to the table. As we sat down, I nodded. "Are you sure you're ready to move? I mean, you weren't last time."

"Yes, I'm ready this time. That was three and a half years ago, Drew. I'm ready now."

"Has your heart healed?"

"My heart will never truly heal. But slowly it is being restored. Grace helps that a lot."

He nodded, then we both seemed to be a loss for words. It hurt, this silence. We'd always been so close, but since the Accident, I had felt him slipping farther and farther away, farther and farther from the man my father had shown him how to be. Maybe that was how he was dealing with his grief, by avoiding it. If I thought he would have listened to me, I would have told him that it would never even begin to heal that way. But, just as I had, he would only learn by experiencing it, not running and hiding. Experience is often the best, and the hardest, teacher.

"What about your heart?" I asked.

He shrugged and looked away. I felt the last grasp on our relationship slip through my fingers. Maybe all we needed was a little time apart, to heal …

More silence, and a knife cut my heart in two, right along the lines of a newly healed scar.

Slowly, I stood up, knowing my heart could take no more of this. I was finally back on my feet again, I had worked through my grief and put it behind me. I couldn't let anything drag me back down, not even my own brother. I knew if I let that happen, I would never be able to get back up.

My brother stood up and walked me to the door. We gave each other a half-hearted hug. He opened his mouth and started to say something, and then closed it again. I stepped out the door, and it took all my will power not to look back. I met Grace and Mandy downstairs. Mandy looked relieved to see that I was leaving, and taking Grace with me. Grace thanked her for the ice cream cone and waved as we left.

The ride back home was quiet. Grace was content with her ice cream cone, which left me with far too much time to think. I wondered if there had been anyway for me to help Drew, before it had gotten this bad. I reflected on the past four years and realized just how much I missed my brother. But I knew I couldn't stay. I'd picked up the broken pieces of my life and put them back together as best I could, for Grace's sake, and then for my own. And now that I was standing on my own two feet again, I knew that I needed a change of scenery.

Chapter 5

By the time we'd arrived at our new house and towed in all the boxes, it was getting dark. I'd cried a little when we'd pulled away from our old house. The moving van had gotten to the new house first and the movers had left everything in the two front rooms. Our new house was only one story, so I could easily push everything into its proper room. Grace was so excited and chit chatted to herself as she wandered amongst the boxes from room to room. It was a cute little house, perfect for the two of us. There were three bedrooms, although the third was more of a large closet. There was a small entryway that led into a living room/dining room area with a fireplace along one wall. It was all hardwood. The kitchen, just off the dining area, was cozy, with a window overlooking a side yard that would be the perfect place for a garden in the spring. The master bedroom was in the back, with another bathroom between the two other rooms. It had a pleasant backyard with a few trees and a fence. It was situated in a quiet neighborhood where the words American Dream were spoken and believed.

I went to bed that night, staring up at the ceiling in the dim light of the moon, believing I had done the right thing, moving here with Grace to start a new beginning, one better than her original beginning. When I looked at Grace, I saw an intelligent, compassionate, happy, young girl who had a bright future. The ghost of my sister no longer stared back at me through the child's eyes, although I still saw my sister through her every day; in her mannerisms, in her smile and the way her eyes lit up with each emotion that passed across her face. I looked around me at the boxes piled high and took in a deep breath. *God, let me stay on the path you have chosen for me*, I prayed. There was a lot of work ahead of me, but as I turned over and shut my eyes, I felt a contentment I hadn't felt in a very long.

The next day, we worked on Grace's room. We painted, moved furniture around and unpacked, although I was doing most of the work with Grace thinking she was helping and her constant stream of chatter. By afternoon on the third day, her room was finished. It looked wonderful, just like the perfect little girl's room. Before we had left Illinois, we had picked up a pale pink to paint the walls, and her bedspread had pink hearts and flowers all over it. She had also picked out a stencil border, and I'd tried my best with the teddy bears and hearts that now danced around her wall just below the ceiling. We had also gotten an area rug for the hardwood floor. Her furniture was all white with a canopy bed that flowed with sheer pink lace. When we were finally finished, she stood in the middle and slowly did a spin, taking in everything with her eyes wide in wonder. She turned to me with a smile so bright it took my breath away.

"I love it, Mommy," she said in a soft voice barely above a whisper. Running over to her bed, she jumped on it, giggling with delight. *If only life were always so simple*, I thought to myself as I watched her. With Grace's room completed, I felt like our house was our home now, even though most everything else was still in boxes.

She took a short nap in her new room, and then we went for a walk around our new neighborhood. The houses were all slightly older, like ours, but had an understated elegance older, well-tended neighborhoods seemed to have. Grace had a way of walking that always seemed almost like dancing to me. "Mommy, do you still have to go to school?" she asked as she skipped along beside me.

"Yes, but I have a couple of weeks to spend with you first," I told her.

"Yea!" Her eyes lit up with excitement. There is something about how excited she gets that has always made me feel special. Watching her skip along and smile, singing a song to herself in the bright summer sun, a sense of contentment continued to spread through me. It seemed that my doubts and fears had melted with the radiance of Grace's smile. I looked down at the beautiful little girl that had been entrusted to my care. I was sure that without her, I wouldn't have been able to find the strength within me to say goodbye to my home, my brother, and my family. Without her, I knew I wouldn't have made it this far. Somehow, having realized this made my soul a little lighter.

All through the next week, as we put our house in order, we had picnics in the parks all around us, we walked around our new neighborhood, and spent a lot of time just having fun together. There were so many new things to see and do and we became expert explorers. Sunday was upon us before we knew it, and I knew we needed to look for a church. I had prayed throughout the week that God's plan would find fulfillment for us in a community. In all our exploring, we had found a beautiful old church a short drive from our house, so we decided to check it out. It looked large, but friendly. As we pulled up, people were calling greetings to one another and laughing as they caught up on a week spent apart. That felt like a good sign to me – and definitely something I knew we needed. Community was the key in our search for a place to worship and belong. I truly believed that was what Grace and I needed to build our new lives in this new place. With all my heart, I also believed God would lead us on His path to fulfillment.

We parked our car and Grace took my hand as we headed up to the building. "It's really pretty, Mommy," Grace said as we walked into the sanctuary, amid greetings from those around us. It had a high ceiling with soft lights hanging down to illuminate the pews. The podium stood in front of a choir loft filled with smiling people in blue robes. A wooden cross hung behind them on the wall, lit by a light from below. There were stain glass windows lining the walls on both sides, causing the sunlight that shone through to appear in brightly colored patterns upon the shiny dark wood of the floor. The windows had small plaques below each one, signifying that each window had been paid for by love in honor of those gone on before us.

"It sure is, Grace. Where would you like to sit?" I quickly deterred her from the front row and we settled down in a pew. After a few minutes, an older man came over to us. He was probably in his 50's, with a balding head and a warm smile.

"Hello. My name is Pastor Jay Hanning. Welcome to our church. Is this your first time here?"

His eyes gleamed with a joyful demeanor and he continued to beam his smile at us, as if he were truly interested in our answer. "Yes, it is. My name is Alyse Sheridon, and this is my daughter, Grace. We just moved to town this week from Illinois, so this is our first Sunday here. You have a very beautiful church."

"Thank you. I do hope that you'll come back again soon." He smiled and started up to the pulpit.

The service was good and the people were very friendly. Several people stopped us and chatted. Many invited us back. I felt truly welcome and took it as a sign of many good things to come according to God's plan for us, my Grace and me.

Chapter 6

The next week we finished up all the unpacking and painting, organizing and putting on the final touches that make a house and home. Each thing was in place, and Grace and I smiled at each other as we walked through our cozy new home.

Friday, we decided to go downtown. Grace needed some new clothes, and I wanted the chance to look around a little. I remembering hearing about the downtown revitalization when I was a teenager and was interested to have a look around, shopping was always a good excuse for exploration. School started on the next week, and I was going to miss my days with Grace.

After navigating ourselves through the city, down Meridian Street past beautiful old mansions with their manicured lawns, and past a Children's Museum I promised Grace we would check out soon, we arrived at a rotary with a monument in the middle. The GPS directed us to continue through the circle and into a parking lot underneath the mall. Grace had been quiet in the back, watching the city pass by her through the window. After we had done our shopping, we stopped at a cute little café for lunch. It was right by the mall downtown, and there were a lot of men and women in suits with briefcases discussing business over submarine sandwiches.

Grace ordered a milkshake and I got an iced tea while we waited for our food. We sat quietly, watching the life around us, when all of a sudden, I heard my name. I didn't know anyone in this big city, so I was sure they must have been talking to another Alyse. Anonymity had been part of the appeal of our new city. But the voice was persistent, and then I heard my last name. Finally, I turned to see a young man walking toward me. He looked strangely familiar.

I sucked in a breath as my emotions ran wild. Devon.

Just as quickly as I'd realized it was him, I realized it was not. Slowly, I stood up.

"Ryan?" I asked as I held out my hand to Devon's younger brother.

"Hi, Alyse." He smiled and I almost started crying but quickly checked my tears. I was much better at that now.

"Ryan, it's good to see you. Please, sit down." He nodded and took a seat. "Grace, this is Ryan. His brother and I used to be good friends when you were a baby."

"This is Grace!" Ryan exclaimed, smiling at my young niece. "This beautiful, big girl can't be the little baby I held in my arms." He winked at me and I couldn't help but smile, despite all the turmoil within me.

"I don't remember you," said Grace, with child-like honesty.

"You were too little to remember," I told her.

"Oh," she replied, and continued to suck on her milkshake. Ryan and I smiled at each other.

"You look really good, Alyse. What are you doing here?"

"We moved here about two weeks ago. I start my new job on Wednesday in a private school. How about you?"

"I have lived here for about a year now, got a job with an ad agency not too far from here after I graduated from college. I like it here, its a good city. How's Drew?" My smile fell, and Ryan picked up on it right away. "If you don't want to talk-"

"No, it's alright. Since the acci – in the past few years, my brother and I seem to have grown apart."

"I'm sorry, Alyse. It's always sad to hear that happen to siblings." He let the conversion drop there, and I knew he wanted to say something about Devon. I really didn't want to ask, but I knew it was the polite thing to do.

"So, how is Devon?" My voice wavered a little, but Ryan didn't seem to notice.

"He's doing pretty well. He is still in Seattle. He says he likes it there, but …" Ryan's voice kind of trailed off and he looked slightly off to the right as if avoiding my eyes. There was an awkward silence.

"But what?" I asked, not wanting to know but also unable to let it go.

"Well, something's missing. I'm not sure he's ever gotten over you." He was looking right into my eyes again.

It took a moment for his words to sink in. Finally, I looked away. I thought about Devon; his laughing eyes, his smile, his strong arms.

"Alyse?" Ryan's voice pulled me back into the present.

"I don't know if I can handle this right now, Ryan."

"Hey, Alyse, I'm sorry." He placed his hand over mine and smiled. "I didn't mean to upset you."

I nodded and looked over at Grace. She looked upset, sensing something from me she couldn't understand. I motioned her over and swung her up onto my lap. It felt so good to hold her close and to know that she loved me. I looked up at Ryan. He had a peculiar look on his face. He noticed me looking at him, and snapped out of it.

"Well, I better get going. Here is my number." He wrote it quickly on a napkin and handed it to me. "I'd really like to stay friends, Alyse. This is a big city," he said, gesturing around him. "It's nice to have good friends to count on."

"Sure, Ryan. That would be nice."

"Great. Well, I'll talk to you later."

"Bye, Ryan."

"Bye, Alyse. Bye, Grace."

She waved and Ryan turned back toward the table from which he had come.

"I have to start school tomorrow," I told Grace as I tucked her in Tuesday evening.

"What will I do?" she asked.

"You'll go to the preschool we visited yesterday. Sound good?"

She nodded and gave me a hug. "Goodnight, Mommy."

"Goodnight, sweetheart. See you in the morning." I kissed her forehead and turned out the lights. I stood outside her door and listened as her breathing evened out. When I knew she was asleep, I walked back in and sat in the chair by her bed. I watched her as she slept, and tears slid silently down my cheeks.

I thanked God daily for the miracle of Grace. Even so, it didn't seem to be enough. It could never be enough. She was the source of my strength, this I knew. And yet, sometimes, I was lonely. I couldn't share everything with Grace. I lived in the world of a four-year-old. I needed adult companionship, but I had shut myself away, telling myself I needed to heal. In my life, I had known a lot of pain and hurt. Sometimes it seemed so much easier to hold everyone at arm's length, or to just push them away completely. I didn't want to hurt anymore, or to hurt anyone else. But I realized enough was enough. I turned and left Grace's room in search of a phone number.

Chapter 7

Over the next few weeks, Grace and I met Ryan for evening picnics and restaurant dates and playtime at local parks. He was very good with Grace, and we enjoyed our time spent with him. He even started going to church with us on Sundays, telling me he had been thinking about looking around for a new one anyway.

Drew actually began emailing me. In these emails, he expressed a desire to change his life. He wrote that after I had left, he'd realized how much he missed me and now he wanted to move ahead in his life, as I had. The realization had finally dawned that what he had been doing was moving so far away from his family emotionally that he could leave to pain behind, but like me, he had found that you have to face it in order to get through it. In my emails to him, I wrote about how proud I was of him and that I was also here for him whenever he needed me.

My job was going great. My class of 17 first graders was terrific and I loved it. At long last, my world seemed to be leveling out and I was actually happy. For the first time in years, I could look around me and say I liked what I saw. I had friends at work. I knew I could always count on Ryan, and we enjoyed each other's company. Grace was thriving at her preschool. My world seemed at peace.

Because of such peace, I kept looking for the crack, the one I was sure my happiness would slip right through. Drew would have told me I was paranoid, but we didn't share like we had in the past.

I thought about Devon a lot, more than I ever would have admitted. Was I over him? Had I really loved him that strongly? Maybe ours had been more of a comfortable love. Had we had true passion? I just couldn't seem to find the answer to my questions. They led me only toward more questions without answers circling ever around the truth I was trying to hard to find … maybe too hard.

At school, there was a teacher who had asked me out a few times. He was handsome and seemed very nice, but so far, I had managed to put him off by not giving him a definite answer and using excuses. I kept reassuring myself that I just wasn't ready. Similarly at church, we had kind people invite us to lunch or playdates and such, but I kindly declined making excuses I kept telling myself were in our best interest.

My life continued this way well into winter.

Grace, Ryan, and I had a quiet Thanksgiving at our house. I had grown to depend on Ryan quite a bit. He was my escape from the world of children. I could talk to him about almost everything. I had people I would call friends, but no really close friends, except Ryan.

The day before Thanksgiving, I received an email from Drew. I decided to wait and share it with Grace and Ryan at dinner. It was something for which to be thankful.

"Grace, I got an email from Uncle Drew yesterday," I told her after we had started our Thanksgiving Day feast. Her eyes widened and a smile lit up her whole face. "He's going to come down to spend Christmas with us!"

"Yea!" she yelled and hopped off her chair to do a little dance around the table.

"That's great news, Alyse," Ryan said. "Now I have something I need to tell you."

"Okay," I replied, waiting. Ryan looked as though he wished he hadn't said anything. "Are you alright?" I asked.

He nodded and looked at Grace. She had returned to her chair and was happily chewing on a piece of turkey. I suddenly began to dread whatever was about to come out of Ryan's mouth, it couldn't be good if he wasn't willing to share it with the congeniality I had come to associate with him.

"Devon is coming out for Christmas," he blurted out then refused to look at me, but continued to watch Grace.

Suddenly, I felt as if I couldn't breath. I grabbed hold of the table for support and continued to watch him. Finally, Ryan looked at me. "Does ... does he know I live here?" I quietly asked.

Ryan solemnly shook his head. "I haven't told him."

"I see. And will you?"

"Do you want me to?"

I didn't answer. I didn't have an answer to give him. Even after four years, I was still trying to straighten it all out in my head, and in my heart.

"Alyse?"

"I don't know, Ryan. I just don't know."

"Maybe if you saw him again you'd know how you felt."

"What if I realize that nothing is there? You said that you don't think he's over me. I don't think I can break his heart twice." I laid my head in my hands and felt the warm tears slip through my fingers.

"Alright, Alyse. I won't say a word to him." Ryan got up from his chair and knelt down beside me. He took my hands and I laid my head on his shoulder. Grace came over and hugged us both.

Chapter 8

"Riiinnngggg!" signaled the bell.

"Children, don't forget the Christmas cards you made today!" I yelled over the noise from the hall. It was the last day before Christmas Break. I watched the children file out and then began the job of tidying up another day's mess. I smiled to myself as I thought about the children's excitement. They were always so alive during the Christmas season.

I gathered up my things and closed up my room. I turned and started toward the outer door. As I walked past the teachers' lounge, several called out "Merry Christmas, Alyse!" I smiled as I continued toward the door to the parking lot. I was still smiling as I picked up Grace and headed home. We sang Christmas carols all the way.

As soon as I unlocked the door, I heard the phone ring. I rushed over and picked it up. "Hello?"

"Hey, Alyse," the voice on the other end said.

"Hey, Ryan."

"I just called to see if you and Grace wanted to go sledding tomorrow."

"Hold on," I told him. I turned to Grace and asked her. Her eyes lit up and she nodded enthusiastically. "Well, I'm not so sure Grace really wants to …"

Grace started jumping up and down, yelling, "Yes, Ryan! Yes, Ryan!" I could hear Ryan chuckling over the phone line. "I guess that's a go," I told him.

"Great. I'll pick you up at 9:30. See you tomorrow."

"Good-bye, Ryan."

Our evening was a quiet one. We added Grace's hand-made decorations from preschool to the tree. We had pizza and watched a Christmas movie, and then it was off to bed to rest up for our exciting day of sledding.

"Thanks for another great day, Ryan," I told him as he drove us home.

"She's quite the little trooper, isn't she?" he said, looking a sleeping Grace in the rear view mirror. "She's always smiling."

I nodded and stared back at my sleeping niece. "She's never been a complainer."

There was a comfortable silence for the rest of the ride home. I was always at ease with Ryan. We got along like Drew and I had in the years before the Accident. I realized how much I had missed such companionship since then. My friendship with Ryan was very important to me.

"Well, here we are," Ryan said as we pulled up in front of my house. "Would you like me to carry Grace into the house?"

"Sure." I got out of the car and followed Ryan and Grace up to the door. After I unlocked it, he headed straight for Grace's room. He helped me helped me take off her shoes and socks and we tucked her in and turned off the light. "Would you like some coffee or hot cocoa before you leave?"

"Sure." He followed me and pulled down two mugs. I set the water on the stove.

"Alyse …"

"Yes, Ryan."

"Are you sure you don't want me to mention you to Devon? Maybe-"

"No, Ryan. I still need to sort through a lot before I see Devon again. I'm just not sure how I feel about him. I haven't really had to deal with it before now, nor did I think I ever really would have to. I just didn't plan on seeing him again."

"But Alyse-"

The teapot rang out shrilly, cutting Ryan off. I turned my back toward him and poured the water into the mugs. After setting the mugs on the kitchen table, I sat down while Ryan sat across from me.

"Do you respect my choice, Ryan?"

"Of course."

"Then you won't say anything to Devon?"

"No, not until you're ready," he replied.

"If I'm ready," I said. "Thank you, Ryan."

We sat there and talked about common everyday things for most of the afternoon. We asked each other's advice and respected each other's opinions. Even the silence was comfortable with him. Finally, Ryan stood up.

"Well, I'd better get going. I'll see you later. Tell Grace I had a great day."

"I'm right here, Ryan," Grace said as she came up behind Ryan and hugged his legs. She giggled as he swung her up into the air.

"I had a great day, Grace. How about you?"

"I had fun!" she exclaimed. Then she turned toward me. "Mommy, can Ryan stay and watch Rudolph with us?"

"That's up to Ryan."

She turned back toward him. "Will you stay?"

"I wouldn't miss it for the world."

"Thank you for putting her to bed," I told Ryan as he came into the kitchen where I was cleaning up.

"No problem. I like doing it."

He helped me finish up, then I walked him to the door. "I had a great day today, Ryan."

"Me, too." He hugged me then headed out to his car.

Chapter 9

"When is Uncle Drew going to get here?" Grace asked.

"Very soon, Grace."

She walked away from the window and crawled into my lap. "How many days until Christmas?" she asked.

"Two."

"Will I get to open my presents then?"

"Yes. Grace, why do we celebrate Christmas?" I asked her.

"Well, baby Jesus was born and we like to celebrate his birthday," she answered.

"And who is baby Jesus?"

"That's easy, Mommy. He is God's Son. Mommy?" she asked.

"Yes, Grace?"

"Does God have any daughters?"

"Well, Grace, all people are God's children, but He has only one true Son, Jesus. We are all God's adopted children."

"What is 'adopted'?" she asked.

I was about to answer her when I felt as if the air had been knocked out of me. How could I explain this to her? She was the perfect example, but I had never told her. "Well, Gracie …" I began, trying to buy myself some time to collect my thoughts. "Adopted means that you are now taking care of something or someone that wasn't yours before. Remember Mr. Fluffy, Mrs. Collins cat? Remember when he came around the house and he was dirty and skinny, and you and Mrs. Collins feed him and he lived in the house with her? He wasn't her cat, but she adopted him, she decided to care for him."

She nodded, "Okay, Mommy," and jumped off my lap to inspect the brightly wrapped gifts under the tree. I took a deep breath and slowly let it out. That's when we heard the car pull up. "Uncle Drew!" Grace yelled and ran toward the door. I handed her coat to her as I pulled mine on and opened the door.

"How are my two favorite ladies?" he asked as he picked Grace up and gave us both a hug.

"I missed you, Uncle Drew," Grace told him and snuggled in closer.

"I missed you, too, Gracie. How about you, sis?"

I smiled at my brother as I realized just how much I had indeed missed him.

"Mommy! Mommy!"

I woke up to someone shaking me and instantly sat up. "What is it? Are you okay, Grace?"

She nodded and her eyes were lit up with excitement. "Is it Christmas Day?" she whispered.

I smiled and nodded my head. "Go wake up Uncle Drew," I told her.

"Okay," she said and flew out of the room.

I put on my robe and headed into the living room in time to see Grace dragging Drew toward the tree. The next hours were spent opening and examining gifts and singing carols and playing games. I watched Grace's face light up with each new discovery and each new delight. It was like watching an angel. We had a late Christmas lunch with all the trimmings. Afterward, Drew took Grace out sledding at the neighborhood park, while I cleaned up.

I was sitting by the fire reading a new book I'd received from Drew when the phone rang. "Hello?"

"Merry Christmas, Alyse," rang out a familiar voice.

"Ryan? Merry Christmas!" I replied. "Wait, how can you be calling me? Does Devon know?"

"No, Alyse. He ran out to get something I'd forgotten for the dinner. I sure do miss your cooking. Be sure to save me some leftovers."

"No problem. Well, have a great Christmas dinner, Ryan."

"Thanks. Um, Alyse, I was wondering what you're doing on New Years Eve, and if you're not doing anything, if you'd like to come with me to an informal gathering one of my colleagues is having."

"Sure, Ryan. I'd love to go with you and meet some of your friends. I'll have to get a babysitter for Grace," I thought out loud.

"Is Drew leaving?" Ryan asked.

"Yes. He leaves the twenty-seventh. How about Devon?"

"The day after. Speaking of Devon, he just pulled up. I've got to go. See you New Year's Eve, say ninish."

"Sounds good. Bye, Ryan."

"Bye."

As I hung up, I thought about what I had just accepted. Did he see it as a date? *No,* I thought to myself, *we're just good friends who enjoy each other's company.* And I didn't think upon it again.

The few days I had with my brother at Christmas were wonderful. He seemed to be more at peace with himself than I had seen him in many years. The evening before he left I had a chance to talk to him about it. Grace had fallen asleep early and Drew and I were enjoying a cup of coffee in the living room, an easy peace between for the first time in a long time. Suddenly, he turned to me.

"Alyse, I've met someone."

"Really? What's she like?" I asked.

"Wonderful," he said and turned back to the large picture window. Soft snow was drifting past. "I realize I haven't made the last few years very easy for you. I want to change my life around. I am tired of running. I've started to go to church with Kristin and I believe now, like you. I am picking up the pieces, following your lead," he said. He turned to me and I could see the familiar twinkle in his eye. "Maybe you should have been the older twin, little sister."

I smiled at my brother, then leaned over and gave him a hug. "I am happy for you. Make sure you give that girl a hug for me."

"I am thinking of going to the police academy this spring. I want to make something of myself, something Dad would be proud of," he told me. "I need to make restitution for what I have done, for myself."

I nodded. "If you are truly turning your life around, then anything you do after that would make Dad proud."

"You really believe that?" he asked.

"Yes, I do."

"Thank you. You have done much for my heart this evening."

"Anytime," I told him. "It feels good to have my brother back."

We sat awhile in companionable silence, watching the weather, each lost in our thoughts. When we parted that night, and again the next day, it was with lighter hearts and a renewed hope in our relationship.

Grace glowed with happiness every time she was the recipient of her uncle's attention. She stayed by his side as much as she could. The day he left, she cried herself to sleep on my lap. I held her tight, and I doubted myself.

I doubted my move to Indianapolis. I doubted my right to have kept Grace and to raise her myself. I doubted my choice to let her call me mom. I held this young, sleeping child in my arms and I cried. This simple release helped my heart relax, and I fell asleep.

Holding her child in my arms, I dreamt of Elizabeth. She smiled at me as we walked through a garden. Flashbacks of our childhood jumped out from beautiful roses in full bloom. She seemed accepting and open with me. We walked toward a small building. She went inside, but would not let me in. She disappeared inside, came back out, handed me a package, then went back inside. When I opened the package, I found Elizabeth's favorite baby doll from when we were children. I looked at the building, and she was smiling at me through the window.

I woke up and Grace was standing beside me. She was smiling again. "Mommy, I drew you a picture," she said and pulled a drawing out from behind her back.

"What a beautiful picture. Is this me?" I asked.

She nodded and climbed into my lap. "And this is me, and that's Uncle Drew."

I gave her a big hug. "Thank you, Grace." I paused a moment as I looked down at my daughter. "How would you like some s'mores?"

"Yeah!" She hopped down and ran into the kitchen.

I smiled as I watched her. "Thank you," I whispered upward, then turned to make a fire in the fireplace to toast, or burn, our marshmallows.

"I'll get it, I'll get it!" Grace yelled as she ran to open the door. It was 8:30 on New Year's Eve.

"Find out who it is first!" I yelled back.

I heard her yell back, "It's Hannah!" Grace took the babysitter's hand and led her into the living room. Hannah was a teenager from our church and Grace loved her.

I left the mirror in my bedroom and headed to the living room. "Hello, Hannah. You know where everything is. Help yourself to whatever. The numbers are on the refrigerator. Grace, would you like Hannah to read to you and tuck you in?"

She nodded. I gave her a big hug and said goodnight, and then Hannah led her off to bed. I finished getting ready and waited for Ryan to pick me up.

Hannah came out a few minutes before nine. "She's sound asleep."

"Thank you, Hannah." We talked for a few minutes, and then I heard Ryan's car. "Have a good evening. I'll be back around 1:00am."

"Bye!"

"Bye, Hannah." I stepped outside onto the porch just as Ryan came up the steps.

"Ready?" he asked.

I nodded and followed him down the steps and got into the car.

"I can't believe we are about to bring in a New Year," Ryan said once we'd gotten into the car.

"It seems to pass so quickly, doesn't it," I remarked. We finished the ride in silence.

The party was at a co-worker's house, and it was decorated brightly for the season with reds and greens prominently displayed. That night, I was introduced to most of Ryan's friends. They all worked for the same ad agency and were all very friendly people. While waiting to ring in the new year, Ryan and I were chatting with two of his colleagues. Actually, they were talking about an account for a large company that they were hoping to get. I was just listening, drifting in and out of the conversation. Suddenly, I realized one of them was talking to me.

"You should consider being a model, Alyse. What do you do?" he asked.

"I'm a teacher. I-"

"You'd be great!" the other man said. "We could hire you to represent one of our clients. What do you think?"

"I don't know. I love teaching and I couldn't give it up," I explained. "Plus there's Grace, but I'm flattered, really."

"You could do it in the summer," Ryan suggested.

"I'll think about it," I said, mostly to pacify them. But I did think about it. I thought about it on the way home and that night in bed. I thought about it the next day. It wouldn't leave my mind.

Grace and I spent the rest of our break together. Ryan called once to thank me for going with him. I could tell he wanted to ask about the modeling idea, but I didn't prompt him at all, so nothing was said.

I started school again and finally had something else to occupy my mind. Over the next couple of weeks, things with Ryan returned to the easygoing attitude of before, he didn't say anything about the modeling. We had dinners, went sledding, and watched movies. We told stories by firelight and roasted marshmallows. Grace absolutely adored Ryan, and he her. We were like a family, and the best of friends. I was thankful that Grace had a man around to spend time with that she and I could trust.

Winter progressed, then brought spring on its heels. For Spring Break, I decided Grace and I should go on vacation.

"How about Florida?" I asked her. She looked up at me with a question written all over her face. "Florida has warm weather," I explained, "and beaches and waves to play in. It also has Disney World and tons of other theme parks."

Her eyes lit up. "Disney World!" she exclaimed.

I nodded. "Shall we go Florida?"

She shook her had enthusiastically, then paused and looked very thoughtful. "Can Ryan come with us?" she asked.

"Oh, not his time, sweetheart." She began to pout, but I looked up at her and smiled. "I thought this could be just a mother/daughter trip. Sound good?"

She smiled again, hugged me, then danced out of the room. Smiling, I did the same.

"All checked in?" he asked.

"Yes," I replied. "Come on, Grace. We don't want to miss the plane." I took her hand and we followed Ryan toward the security line. "Thanks again for driving us here," I told him.

"No problem. I wanted to see my two favorite ladies off to Florida." He took Grace's other hand and smiled at me. "And I'll be here to pick you up Saturday."

"Thanks," I told him.

"Be sure to take lots of pictures for me, okay Gracie," Ryan said.

"I will, Ryan," she said. She tugged on his hand until he was looking down at her. "I wanted you to come, too, but Mommy said no," Grace said innocently.

I turned toward Ryan and could feel the color rising in my cheeks. "Well, I - uh … said that – I … oh, my … that this was a mother/daughter vacation and that maybe-"

"It's okay, Alyse," he said, laughter filling up his eyes and threatening to spill out his mouth as the corners of his lips twitched. I looked at his face with a sheepish grin. "Maybe we could go camping this summer," he said, still looking at me.

"Oh, goody," Grace said.

We arrived at the line and Ryan stood with us as inched forward. Finally, we were next to hand our tickets to the security officer and Ryan could go no further with us.

"Okay, Grace, ready?" She nodded and took my hand.

"Bye, Ryan," Grace and I said as he stepped out of line and I handed our tickets over for inspection. Grace walked on ahead of me and I turned and saw Ryan one last time before turning toward the inspection line.

Chapter 10

Grace and I had a wonderful vacation. We spent a lot of time on the beach playing in the water and sand. We built sandcastles and sand animals. There was sand in our rental car and hotel room. I teased Grace that we would probably take half the beach home with us.

We visited all the tourist spots and a few extras. After a week outside in the sun, we both had great tans and lighter hair. Grace's eyes shone with health and happiness. We had to buy an extra suitcase for all the souvenirs we'd picked up. Grace didn't want to leave, but I mentioned Ryan picking us up and she smiled and readied for our trip home.

On the plane ride home, I thought about our wonderful mother/daughter week. I also wondered how long it would be before Grace asked about her father. I had often doubted my decision to let her call me mom, but Drew and Devon had backed the decision to allow her, so I had tried to put my doubts aside. I had legally adopted her, so she was my daughter, but she was also my niece. What was I going to tell her?

"I can't wait to show Ryan everything we got," Grace told me. She smiled and then turned back toward the window.

When we landed, we got off the plane and headed toward baggage. On the way down the escalator, I saw Ryan immediately. He was standing at the bottom of the escalator at the head of the crowd holding flowers. I pointed Grace toward him and she jumped off the last step of the escalator and ran the few steps remaining toward him. He swung her up into his arms and came forward.

"These are for you and Grace. Welcome home," he said, handing me the flowers.

"Thank you, Ryan." I took the flowers and started with him toward the baggage claim. Grace told him all about the trip while we waited for our bags and all the way home. Ryan listened patiently and asked a few questions. When we got back to the house, I ordered a pizza for dinner while Grace showed Ryan all her new souvenirs.

After dinner, I put Grace to bed, then headed back out to the living room.

"She sure had a great trip, didn't she."

I nodded and sat down. "Thanks for listening to her, Ryan. I really appreciate how good you are with her."

"She's a great kid, Alyse. You've done a good job raising her by yourself."

"Thank you."

"What's on your mind, Alyse?" Ryan asked.

"Nothing."

"I know you better than that, Aly. You've been quiet tonight. Do you want to talk about it?" he asked. He turned toward me on the couch. "You know you can talk to me about anything."

I nodded and stared out the window. After taking a deep breath, I turned back to him. "Ryan, I need your honest opinion. You're my best friend and I know I can count on you." I paused and searched his familiar face as I asked, "Should I tell Gracie the truth?"

His honest, open expression didn't change as he contemplated my question. "Does she know you're her aunt?"

I hung my head down and slowly shook it. "That's what I'm asking you. Should I tell her? Will she want to call me Aunt Alyse? I don't think I can take that. Not now, not after so long. Will it cause more trauma than it is worth? I should have already told her, I guess. I've adopted her. Legally, I am her mother. Oh, I just don't know what to do."

Ryan leaned forward and wrapped his arms around me. I held on tight for a few moments, until my confusion settled and flowed out of me. Then, I pulled back. Ryan looked into my eyes and smiled.

"When the time comes, Aly, you'll know what to do. You are a great mother."

"Thanks, Ryan." We sat for a few moments in companionable silence. Then we stood up and I walked him to the door. He gave me a quick hug, then headed out to his car.

The next day Ryan picked us up for church, as usual. We dropped Grace off at her Sunday school class and then headed to ours. After the church service, the pastor walked up to Ryan and me and introduced us to a family that was new to the area.

"Alyse, Ryan, this is Alex and Jillian Archer. They moved into the house down the block from you," he told us.

"Oh, yes. Hello," I said. Ryan and I shook their hands. I wondered where Pastor Jay was going with this.

"The Archers have three children. Their youngest is Grace's age and they were looking for a good preschool and daycare. I know that Grace loves where she is, and thought maybe you could tell them about it. You could carpool." Pastor Jay smiled at me, then turned to greet some others.

"Why don't you come over and have lunch with us. We can talk about Grace's preschool then, if you'd like," I offered.

"That would be great," Jillian said. I told her my house number and she said they'd be over in about half an hour.

"I hope you don't mind my inviting them over," I told Ryan as we walked downstairs to pick up Grace.

"No problem, it is your house," he told me. I smiled then turned to open the door to Grace's room.

"Mommy!" she yelled and ran over.

"Ready?"

She nodded. I grabbed her coat and we headed to the car. "Grace," I began, "we are going to have some company for lunch. They're the family that bought the house down the street from us. Pastor Jay introduced us after church. Okay with you?"

"Uh-huh," she replied.

Ryan pulled up to our house and we went inside. I began lunch while Ryan helped Grace change out of her church clothes. "Make sure they match," I called out after him. When Ryan and Grace came back into the kitchen I went and changed. Ryan, Grace, and I finished making lunch together. It was a Sunday afternoon tradition.

When we were almost finished, the doorbell rang. "I'll get it," Grace said and ran toward the door. Ryan smiled at me and followed her.

"Thanks," I called out after him. I pulled the pasta off the stove and headed for the door. "Hello," I greeted the Archers as they came in. Grace backed up against me. "Jillian, Alex, this is my daughter, Grace. Grace, this is Jillian and Alex. They live down the street."

"Hello, Grace," Jillian said. "This is Aaron and Kyle. This is my daughter, Courtney. She was in your class this morning."

"Why don't you show Courtney your room, Grace," I said and gently pushed her forward. "You can show her what you got in Florida." Grace stepped forward and took Courtney's hand. We watched them disappear into the hallway. "Lunch is almost ready. Why don't you sit down, make yourselves comfortable until then," I said.

"Come on into the living room," Ryan said. He took the Archers' coats and laid them on a chair. Alex and his sons followed him into the living room.

"I can help you, if you'd like," Jillian volunteered.

"Thanks." She followed me into the kitchen. Jillian set the table while I finished putting everything together. "I think we're ready."

"Thanks for inviting us into your home. We just moved here last week and we don't know anyone. Alex's company transferred him here," Jillian explained.

"Where are you from?" I asked.

"Wisconsin, over an hour north of Chicago. Alex has some family about an hour west of here, close to the Illinois. Other than that, we don't know anyone around here." she answered.

"It's a good city. It won't take long to learn your way around and make it your own," I told her from experience. I turned and headed into the living room. "Lunch is ready," I announced.

Everyone made their way to the table while I got the girls. Lunch was pleasant. I told Jillian about the preschool Grace attended. She said she'd love to check it out. Her boys started at the public school on Monday. Aaron was in third grade and Kyle was in second. After lunch, Alex and Ryan took the kids to the playground while Jillian and I cleaned up.

"Excellent lunch, Alyse."

"Thanks. Thank you for helping me," I said.

"Your husband is very good with children," Jillian told me.

"Ryan? He's not my husband," I said, turning away from Jillian and walking back to the table.

"Oh, I'm sorry," she replied, clearly at a loss for words.

The silence was awkward, but I wasn't sure I wanted to explain. So far, I liked Jillian but I wasn't ready to make her my confidante. I gathered up the rest of the plates and headed back into the kitchen. The curiosity was written all over her face and I could tell Jillian wanted to question me. I set the plates down and turned back to her,leaning back against the counter.

"He's my best friend, but not my husband. We moved here last July, Grace and me. We ran into Ryan one afternoon. His brother and I were friends several years back. Anyway, he's been a great help with Grace and a good friend. Grace adores him."

Jillian smiled at me and I wondered what she was thinking. While we cleaned up, Jillian told me about her old life and the move. She opened right up to me. It made me long to open up to her as well, to be able to drop the curtain of caution with another human being – a woman! - but something held me back. It might have been that old fear of hurting and being hurt that I thought I had long ago worked through, but I didn't want to stop to analyze just then.

When we were done, Jillian and I sat down on the sofa in the living room and continued our chat. She asked about my job, and I asked about hers. She was looking for a job and had a degree in nursing.

Later that evening, after the Archers had left and Grace was in bed, Ryan was preparing to leave. "I like the Archers," he told me.

"Me, too," I replied.

"Looks like we have gotten ourselves some new friends," Ryan said with a confident smile. He gave me a quick hug and headed out to his car.

Chapter 11

"Did you have a good day today?" I asked Grace and Courtney after school on

Thursday. The Archers had had us over for dinner Tuesday, and Jillian asked me if I could baby-sit Thursday afternoon. She had a job interview, but said she'd be home by five.

The girls giggled from the back seat. They had become best friends very quickly. When we pulled up in front of the Archers' house, I could see the boys down the street, walking home after school.

"Can we go to your house, Alyse?" Courtney asked.

"Let's ask the boys," I told her. Aaron and Kyle agreed and we left a note for Jillian. We spent our afternoon playing games. After Jillian had picked up her children, Grace and I made dinner and sat down to eat.

"Why don't I have any brothers?" Grace asked me. I braced myself for the conversation I'd been dreading for awhile now.

"Well, Grace," I paused, not sure what to say. "You need a mommy and a daddy to have a baby."

She thought about that one for a minute while she chewed on a bite of pasta. "Is Ryan my daddy?"

I stared at Grace Elizabeth and couldn't answer. Is that what she thought? *Well,* I told myself, *and why not. She's just a child. She doesn't understand.* How could I explain it to her? "No, Grace. Ryan is not your dad, he is a friend of ours."

She looked hurt. "Doesn't he want to be my daddy?" she asked, tears beginning to fill her eyes.

"I'm sure he would love to be your daddy, Grace. But it doesn't work that way."

"Why not?" she innocently asked.

"Well, because, uh … mommies and, uh … daddies have to be … married," I told her.

"Why aren't you and Ryan married, then he could be my daddy," she told me, her young mind fast at work with child-like logic. To her, it was that easy.

"Because Ryan and I are friends, Grace. We do fun things together, but then he goes home." I must have sounded frustrated because she just said, "Oh," and continued to eat her food, looking quite confused. From then on, our evening was quiet. After I put Grace to bed, I called Ryan.

"Hello?"

"Ryan …"

"Alyse, what's wrong? Is Grace okay?"

I nodded, then realized he couldn't see me. "Yes, but she asked tonight, Ryan. I tried to explain, but I think I only confused her more." As I said it, I felt held-in tears begin to escape. It seemed I was always crying about something. I was growing quite tired of it.

"Asked about what, Aly?" he asked me.

"Her father," I whispered.

"I'll be right over."

I sat outside on the front porch until I saw Ryan's car. He came flying out of the car and ran up the walk. He started to open the screen door before he saw me. He held out his arms and I fell into them. We stood outside for awhile, then he led me inside.

"I don't know what to do, Ryan," I whispered. "I just want to do what's best for her, I want her to have a good, happy life with all the best I can provide. I want her to be okay. I don't know what to do!"

We sat down on the sofa. Ryan tilted my face up and looked into my eyes. He wiped my tears away. "You are a good mother, Alyse. Grace is just confused right now. She looks around her and sees moms and dads and brothers and sisters and it confuses her. It's going to make her wonder."

I nodded and leaned against Ryan. What he said made sense to me and the way he said, his voice full of confidence and serenity, it calmed the storm inside. I closed my eyes and Ryan took my hand. We sat silent for awhile, then he began to tell me a funny story about work, and before long, my problem seemed smaller and there was a smile on my face. Ryan just seemed to have that effect.

Chapter 12

"Ready?" I asked Grace. She nodded.

"Let's head out then, " Ryan said. "Are we meeting the Archers there?"

"Yes. Do you have the food?" I asked Ryan.

"Yeah. Come on, Grace. Let's go." He held the door open and we headed out to the car. When we arrived at the park, the Archers were already there. We added our food to theirs and the children took off toward the playground.

"The first picnic of the season," Ryan remarked.

"A promise of many more to come, I hope," Jillian said.

I smiled and turned to Ryan. "I'm going to play with Grace."

"I'll walk with you," he said.

"Bring them back with you when you're done," Jillian called after us. "We're almost ready to eat."

Ryan and I walked toward the playground. When Grace saw us, she came running over. "Will you push me on the swings, Ryan?" she asked.

"Sure," he told her.

"Me, too?" asked Courtney.

"Of course, " he said.

"You have your own daddy," Grace told her. "Ryan," she said, turning back to him, "only push me, okay." Grace started off toward the swings and Courtney started walking back to the picnic area. Ryan turned to me.

"Talk to Courtney, "I told him. I headed for the swings. Grace was crawling up into one. As soon as she was situated, I knelt down in front of her. "Grace, why did you say that to Courtney?"

"It's true. She has her own daddy. Ryan is mine, not hers. So he should push me."

"Grace, do you remember what I told you about Ryan? He's is not your daddy. He is our friend," I tried to tell her again.

She nodded then looked up at me. "Can he be my daddy, for pretend?"

Her eyes looked so innocent I didn't know what to say. Her eyes switched from mine to something behind me. I turned and saw Ryan. He knelt down next to me and smiled, then turned toward Grace.

"Grace, I'm your friend, you know that, right?"

She nodded. "That's what Mommy says."

"And you know I love you very much," he continued.

Again, she nodded.

"I'll always be here for you, no matter what. Friends do that for each other. If you need me, just let me know. Can I have a hug?"

A smile lit my daughter's face as she gave Ryan a hug. "My turn," I said. She gave me a hug, too. "Ready to eat?"

"Yeah!" She crawled out of the swing and took Ryan's hand to lead us over to the picnic area.

"Thanks," I mouthed to Ryan over Grace's head.

He just smiled.

"Before I leave, Alyse, I wanted to ask you about something," Ryan told me that night. We'd had dinner and put Grace to bed. Now we were on the front porch, and Ryan was about to leave.

"What is it, Ryan? If it's about Grace and this afternoon, then-"

"No, Alyse. It's not that."

"What, then?" I asked.

He walked over to the porch swing and sat down. I followed. "We just picked up an account last week for a perfume company. They're expanding to shampoo and soap and the like. My team is working on their advertising, and we'll be ready to shoot in about a month, around the time school is out. My team and I feel you would be perfect for the job."

"I don't know, Ryan," I told him.

"What's holding you back? You're out of school. It won't take the whole summer, you'll still have time with Grace. Its mostly print ads. You can bring her with you and I'll help you watch her. Jillian's only working part time. She could watch her some. Won't you at least think about it?"

"Yeah, I'll think about it," I told him.

I watched Ryan's car pull away, and a million thoughts were running through my head. I was flattered they wanted me as their model. Ryan told me they would still have to run it by some people for approval if I agreed. It was an exciting proposition. *I would love to work with Ryan, to see him at the job and understand a little better what it was he did,* I told myself. So what was holding me back? I couldn't pinpoint it, other than a thrill of fear at the prospect of putting myself out there for the attention of others. *You think far too much for your own good*, I told myself, then turned in for the night.

May flew by. Before I knew it, it was the last week of school. I stared out at my students and reflected on my first year in Indianapolis. Ryan had been the best thing about the move. He was a very important part of my life now. He was my best friend and he was so good to me and to Grace. She had flourished in the past year. Even though we'd had problems, Grace and I had become a family even more than before. And Drew and I were finally repairing what had long since been broken by the Accident. He was getting married in July and he wanted Grace and me to come up for it. He was going to graduate from the police academy soon and start a new life and career. I was so proud of him.

The bell pulled me out of my reverie. "Good-bye, children," I called, "see you tomorrow."

I drove by Jillian's on my way home to pick up Grace. It was her week to pick the girls up from preschool. The Archers were another great thing in my life. Jillian and I had become good friends in the two months she'd lived down the street from me. I had finally been able to open up and share a part of myself with another person, it felt so wonderful to have a true girlfriend.

"Hello!' she said when she opened the door.

"Hello, Jillian," I replied.

"Mommy," Grace yelled and threw herself into my arms.

"Hey, sweetie. How was your day?"

"Good." Her smile lit up my day.

"Go get your things, Grace." She nodded and ran off in search of her belongings. Jillian invited me in.

"Do you know what you're going to tell him, yet?" she asked.

"I think I'm going to accept the job."

"Alyse, that's wonderful!" Jillian exclaimed.

"He has to know by tonight. If I take it, I'll start next week. I'll be done by July, in time for my brother's wedding, and a little vacation time with Grace."

By then Grace was ready to go. We headed home and began preparations for dinner. Ryan was coming over, and tonight I was going to give him my answer.

"That was delicious, Alyse. You should be a chef," Ryan said. Grace helped us clear the table, and then Ryan and I set about to do the dishes.

"Ryan," I started. "I decided to take the job. I could use the extra money, and I'll be done by July for Drew's-"

"You're saying yes?" Ryan repeated.

I nodded. He looked at me with a funny expression on his face, then threw his arms around me and swung me around, not caring that his hands were flinging soapy water everywhere.

"I'm so glad! You're going to love it, Alyse, I promise. It'll be great."

Ryan looked so excited. He continued to talk as we finished the dishes. He attempted to explained everything to me and some.

School ended that Friday. Grace and I went out for a mother/daughter evening in celebration of the coming summer. Saturday, we watched cartoons together and made cookies. Ryan came over and we went for a picnic then out to a movie, a basic lazy Saturday, but quite enjoyable. Courtney came over and we played games until dinnertime. Then the babysitter arrived and Ryan and I went out to celebrate my new job. He had insisted on taking me out. I quickly changed, then headed out into the living room.

"Ready?"

"Yes, lets go," I replied and then turned to my daughter. "Goodnight, Grace. Be good for Hannah. Love you."

"Bye, Mommy," she said, "bye, Ryan." She gave us both a hug, then headed off to read with Hannah.

Ryan, Courtney, and I walked out to the car. We dropped Courtney off on the way. I got out and walked her to the door. "Have fun," Jillian said as she ushered Courtney inside.

I got back into the car. "Alright," I said as I fastened my seat belt. "Where are we going?"

"It is a surprise," he told me, a mischievous grin on his face. We ended up at my favorite restaurant. It was so nice to have an adult evening, to be able to sit and enjoyed my meal and my company. Afterward, Ryan dropped me off.

"Thank you, Ryan. I had a wonderful evening." I leaned over, gave him a quick kiss on the cheek, then started to get out of the car.

"Wait, Alyse," Ryan said as he put his hand on my arm. I turned back to look at him, but I could not see his face in the darkness.

"What is it, Ryan?" I asked.

He paused. "Never mind,' he said softly.

"If you change your mind, you know where I live, okay?" I half joked. I could see the slight movement of his head nodding, then his hand slipped off my arm. "Goodnight, Ryan," I said, slightly confused but trying not to let it show.

"Goodnight," he replied softly.

Chapter 13

Monday morning I was incredibly nervous as I helped Grace get dressed. Now that school was out, Jillian had volunteered to watch Grace on Mondays, Wednesdays, and Fridays.

"Are you going to school today, Mommy?" she asked me.

"I am going to work with Ryan now, and you're going to stay at Courtney's when her mommy isn't working. School is out for the summer and in the fall, you get to go to kindergarten, remember?" The smile lit up her face and her eyes as she nodded.

After chit chattering with me the entire way down the street about school and Courtney, I dropped her off at the Archers' then headed into the city. As I made my way into the building, my stomach felt full of butterflies and my hands shook. By the time I knocked on Ryan's office door I could barely stand still. I had to keep reminding myself why I was doing this – I knew I needed to push myself to try new things, that was something my dad had always had to remind me to do. That thought gave me just enough courage to continue forward when Ryan called - "Come in." I pushed the door open, stepped inside, and fell into the closest chair. "Alyse," Ryan said, standing up to shut the door. "Are you okay?"

"How did I ever let you talk me into this?" I asked, a half crazed laugh caught in my throat.

"You'll be fine, no-you'll be great. You stand in front of a classroom everyday," he tried to reassure me.

"Those are children, Ryan. I'm a teacher, I know what I'm doing in a classroom. I do not know what I am doing here, though."

Ryan knelt down beside me and took my hand. "Alyse, I'll be here the whole time. You'll be fine, I promise. Trust me?"

"Of course," I told him, squeezing his hand. I took a deep breath and stood up. "Okay. We'd better go before I change my mind." Ryan smiled and opened the door for me.

He spent the morning introducing me to all the people I'd be working with and familiarizing me with everything I'd need to know. It was quite confusing. Then, he took me out to lunch, to the same café where he'd spotted Grace and me our first week in the area.

After lunch, we began shooting, just for practice, to get me used to it. Over the next two weeks, we shot everything they needed. Grace came with me a few times. She was such a little ham. She loved the cameras so the photographers shot some pictures of her as well, just for fun. She loved it.

As we finished up the last week, I looked back on my experience. It had been a little scary, but what stood out the most was my time spent with Ryan. We'd had lunch almost every day, and I enjoyed working with him and spending time with just him.

As the week drew to a close, I looked forward to the camping trip we were going on with the Archers. It was sort of a celebration for a job well done. We were also celebrating Grace's fifth birthday.

We were technically done Thursday, but we had a small party Friday morning to wrap it all up. I brought Grace into the office with me. The crew all greeted her and a few pretended to tickle her. She laughed and giggled and chatted with everyone. She loved the attention.

One of the cameramen approached me while I was making a plate for Grace out of the party food. "You have a great daughter," he told me.

"Thanks," I told him.

"She's going to be a beauty, just like her mom," he said, then his face flushed as if he had just figured out what he'd said. He grinned at me sheepishly.

"Thanks," I said again. He nodded, grabbed a handful of chips and walked away. I was still smiling when Ryan walked over.

"All set for tonight?" he asked.

I nodded. "Grace and I are going to pick up a few last minutes supplies on the way home today."

"Good," he said, then leaned against the table, following my eyes as I searched for Grace. I found her and could hear her talking to an older lady about how her Mommy usually went to school, but that she didn't have to for awhile. Then I heard her tell the lady she was going camping. "She's so at home everywhere, Aly," I heard Ryan whisper beside me. I nodded again, not needing words to describe how I felt when my face said it all, and Ryan was a good reader, anyway. "Everyone has been telling me what a good sport she is and how well behaved she was when you were shooting, and how friendly, how pretty, it goes on and on. You have a real treasure in that child."

"Thank you, Ryan. You know, you have really helped her in the last year. She was excited to move, but I think you have made it easier for her to be so far from her uncle. Thank you, although those words don't quite seem adequate to convey how appreciative I truly am."

"It was my pleasure, Alyse … it always has been," he finished softly, an odd tone in his voice. He quickly walked away before I could ask him about it, I was left watching him and wondering what had gotten into him.

"Are you excited about our camping trip?" I asked her as we pulled out into traffic.

She nodded her head eagerly. "When do we leave?"

"We have to go to the grocery store first," I told her. "Then, when Ryan comes by, we'll go to the Archers' and start out."

"Yea!" she exclaimed. I smiled over at her as we pulled into the parking lot of the grocery store. After we'd stocked up on all the camping food – like hot dogs, marshmallows, and chocolate bars, all the important stuff – we headed home to pack.

"Grace, will you be my lookout?" She nodded and smiled. "Watch for Ryan." She turned toward the window and started singing a song to herself. I smiled and turned toward the bedrooms. I was just finishing up when Grace came bounding into the room.

"He's here!" she yelled. "Can we go now?"

"Let him in," I told her, then followed her out to the living room. Grace raced to the door and opened it just in time for Ryan to walk right in. She threw her arms around him.

"Let's go," she told him.

"Hello to you, too," Ryan laughed. She let go of his legs and grabbed his hand, trying to tow him back outside. "We need to get your bag for the trip, Gracie." She let go of his hand and ran for her room. "So, Alyse," he said, turning to me, "how does it feel to be done with the print ads and the commercial clips?" he asked.

"It feels good," I replied. "It was fun but I'm ready to get on with my summer."

"They're wonderful. You're wonderful. Everybody loves the clips," Ryan told me.

"I'm glad. Are we ready to go?"

"Yes!" Grace called from her room. She came back in dragging her bags behind her.

"I'll get the rest," I said and headed off to my bedroom. Ryan picked up Grace's bags and headed out to his vehicle. Since he drove a 4x4 sport utility, we were taking it instead of my car. When we had it all packed, we headed down to the Archers'.

"It's going to be a great weekend," Ryan said. "We'll get some rest and relaxation."

"And fun!" Grace added.

"Of course," Ryan said, "anything you say, Doll." He smiled over at me as he pulled out from in front of our house and headed down the street.

Courtney joined us for the ride to the campsite. The girls sang and giggled the whole way there. When we finally pulled in, it was beginning to get dark.

"Let's go ahead and start a fire," Alex said. He sent his boys out looking for small twigs while he and Ryan set up the tents. After they had the fire going, we roasted some hot dogs and marshmallows.

"Will you tell us a scary story?" Aaron asked his dad.

"Yeah!" Kyle added. "Please, Dad."

I looked over at the girls. Courtney looked excited, but she had been camping and heard some of her dad's stories already. Grace looked terrified. "Grace, sweetie, why don't you come sit in my lap." She nodded and came over.

Ryan sat down beside me. "Tents are all secure," he said.

"Mommy, can I sit in Ryan's lap?" Grace asked me.

"Sure, if it's okay with Ryan." I tried to keep the hurt out of my voice. She turned to Ryan. He smiled and pulled her over onto his lap.

Alex started with a mild story about two lost travelers. It didn't take long for Grace and Courtney to fall asleep, and after they did, he told scarier stories. Without realizing it, I slid closer to Ryan. Alex's stories weren't really that scary, but next to Ryan I felt safer, and warmer. After awhile, he slid his arm out and around me, and I leaned against him and began to grow tired.

We retired to our tents soon after. Jillian, Courtney, Grace, and I slept in one and the guys slept in the other. Ryan gently laid Grace down on her sleeping bag. "Thanks, Ryan," I said.

"No problem." He smiled then headed to the other tent. "Goodnight, Alyse."

"Goodnight, Ryan."

After breakfast the next day, we all went out for a hike. The countryside was wonderful and the fresh air felt good. The children ran around in front of us. Then Courtney got tired of walking so Alex gave her a piggyback ride. Grace didn't want one, though Ryan offered. Instead she walked along between us, holding our hands and swinging our arms, humming to herself and laughing at the boys.

The boys ran ahead to investigate something and Courtney decided she wanted down. She didn't want to be left out of anything her brothers were doing. Grace joined her and the two girls went bounding after the boys with warnings from us to stay within view and on the trail. As we walked along, Ryan slid closer and took the hand Grace had just freed. He smiled and continued walking. My hand felt comfortable in Ryan's grasp and I didn't think anything of it.

A little further down, there was a small trail leading off our main trail. A sign next to it said it led to a small lake. "Alyse, let's head down and see the lake," Ryan suggested, pulling me toward the small trail.

"Sure. Grace," I yelled.

"Just us," Ryan said. "I'm sure Alex and Jillian will watch Grace."

"No problem," Jillian said in response.

"Well, okay," I said, "but not for long."

Ryan and I walked along in silence. The foliage was denser along this trail. Then we stepped out of the foliage onto the shore of the small lake. Everything was so peaceful. "There's a bench right over there," Ryan said, pointing to my left.

"We should head back, Ryan."

"Just sit with me for a few minutes, enjoy the still peacefulness." He led me over to the bench and we sat down. I took a deep breath of the clean, cool air and closed my eyes. It was nice not to hear children yelling; only nature's voice carried on the soft breeze. I opened my eyes and glanced over at Ryan. He was staring at me.

"You're so beautiful, Alyse," he said softly.

I didn't know how to respond. Slowly, he leaned over and his lips met mine. I closed my eyes and he slid closer and wrapped his arms around me. Arms that had held me a hundred times, arms I'd looked to and needed, now held me in a different way.

Something in my brain clicked and I panicked and pulled away. I jumped back off the bench and froze as emotions from pleasure through to anger swept through my body. Ryan jumped up as well.

"Alyse," he said, "I'm sorry."

I just stood there and stared at him. He took a step closer, but I couldn't move, my feet felt planted to the ground.

"Alyse," Ryan said, and took another step closer. He took hold of my hand, and put his other hand on my cheek. "I've wanted to do that for a long time." He looked deep into my eyes and I could see what my eyes held reflected back at me through his, pain and love and shock. "I love you," he said so softly I almost didn't hear. Again he brought his lips to my mine. I remained frozen for just a few seconds, but once I regained control, I tore away from him and turned toward the lake. My breathing was ragged and I was shaking all over. I could feel his presence behind me.

"Alyse, look at me."

I shook my head as the tears began to form in my eyes. I felt panic flowing through every fiber of my being and I had to get away. Ryan reached for me and I felt his hands on my arms. I broke loose and ran back up the trail. I heard him yelling after me but I didn't stop. I needed time to think so I took the long way back to camp.

When I got back to camp, I didn't see Ryan. Jillian came running over. "Alyse, what's wrong? What happened?"

I just shook my head.

"Let's go for a walk. Alex can watch the children."

"Where's Ryan?"

"He came through here a bit ago. He got in his vehicle and drove off. He looked really upset. Do you want to talk about it?" Jillian asked.

I nodded and she led me down a short trail to a small clearing with a few picnic tables. We sat down at one and I put my head in my hands and sobbed. Jillian put her hand on my arm and waited until I was ready to talk. When I was, I told her what had happened.

"Alyse," she said, and I turned to look at her face. She had a gentle smile. "You never noticed anything before this?"

I shook my head.

"I noticed the first day I met you two. It's the way he looks at you, the way he touches you, and his smile. He brightens up whenever you are around. You've never noticed?" she asked again, her voice gentle.

I shook my head. "I don't know what to do."

"Do you love him?"

"Well, yes. He's my best friend. But I don't know if I love him the way he loves me." I stared up at the sky and felt even more confused than before.

"Just sit and think about it for awhile. See if you haven't buried something deep in your heart," she said.

Without thinking, the whole story of Devon poured out of my heart and out of my mouth, a story I hadn't shared with anyone in years, if ever. I spared Jillian no details and felt completely drained when I was finished. With my eyes closed, I whispered, "I'm afraid."

"Of what?" she asked gently.

"Hurt, pain, rejection, of hurting someone else again," I said slowly.

"Those are all a part of life, Alyse. We live, we learn, we make mistakes and we search for answers. What if you don't take the risk and Ryan's the one you've been waiting for, the one you are meant to be with? You'll regret that you didn't try. Do you want to look back and wonder what might have been?"

I looked at Jillian. She was smiling gently again, and I wanted desperately to believe what she was saying. I just didn't know how. Or maybe I did, I just didn't want to face it. It would mean pushing out of my comfort zone and taking a risk with the ever present possibility of getting hurt.

We sat there in silence for awhile. Finally, Jillian stood up. "I need to head back. Take all the time you need, Alyse. Grace will be fine."

I nodded and she headed back to camp, which left me alone with my thoughts. How did I feel about Ryan? I wanted to talk to him about this, like we'd talked about everything, but things were different now. Suddenly, I was angry with him for doing this. But my anger burned out quickly, I just couldn't imagine my life without him. He was my best friend. In the end, it all boiled down to one question: Was I in love with Ryan?

"You think too much," I told myself. I got up off the bench and headed back to the campground.

I saw Ryan as soon as I got back to camp. He was kneeling down in front of Grace, saying something I was too far away to hear. She nodded and gave him a hug. He saw me over her shoulder and quickly stood up as Grace turned to see what was behind her.

"Mommy!" she called and ran over to me.

"Hi, sweetheart." I swung her up into my arms. "My, you're getting so big." I held her close for a few seconds, then set her back down on the ground.

"Mommy, Ryan says he's leaving now," she said. "Tell him to stay." She took my hand and began to tow me over to where Ryan was standing.

"Grace, Ryan and I need to talk."

"Will you make him stay?" she asked me, looking up at with my sister's eyes.

"Go play, Grace," I told her, gently turning her around. I couldn't look into those innocent eyes a moment longer without breaking down. It took all my courage but I looked up into Ryan's face. "You leaving?" I tried to ask causally, but I couldn't pull it off.

"I'm not sure I am welcome here anymore," he told me.

At the sound of his voice my traitorous heart leaped up in my chest. I looked down at my hands quickly, knowing I couldn't respond without losing control.

"Do you want me to stay?" he asked softly.

Again I felt myself wanting to say yes, but not knowing how. I was taken back in time to a room with a cozy fireplace and a ring on my finger. And yet, how far had I really come? I still didn't know what I wanted. Or did I?

I felt hands on my face, tilting it up. His eyes searched my face for something, anything. "Do you want me to stay?" he asked again.

"Do you want to go?" I asked, barely whispering, hoping, wanting, afraid of both.

"No," he replied firmly. He was so sure of what he wanted. And I … I wasn't.

"I'm not sure what to think. This is all so sudden. I … I-"

"You never suspected anything?" he asked. He hands slipped from my face to take hold of my hands.

I shook my head.

"Oh, Alyse, I've loved you for so long, since you were my brother's girlfriend. I thought he was so lucky to have you. But, I fell in love with you sometime last fall on all those picnics and play dates. Because I love you so much, I want you to be happy. That's why I wanted you to see Devon again, so I would know if I had a chance with you, or if … or if you'd go back to him," he finished quickly, never looking away from my eyes.

"Ryan, I don't want to hurt you. You're my best friend. But I need some time to sort everything out. We need to slow down. I …"

He stepped forward and took me in his arms, effectively cutting of my meandering thought. I cried on his shoulder, as I had so many times before. "I don't want to lose you," I whispered.

"You'll never lose me," he whispered back.

The duration of the camping trip was a little awkward for me whenever Ryan was near. I wasn't sure how to act around him anymore, and I still hadn't sorted out how I felt.

Alex led our devotions Sunday morning. At lunch we had a birthday party for Grace. She glowed with the attention. My daughter was definitely a people person, like my sister had been. We ate cupcakes I had brought for the occasion, sang to her, and let her open her presents.

Afterward, we packed up and headed home. Jillian and I were packing up the girls' things when she turned to me.

"Alex's family always has a huge gathering for the Fourth of July. Do you guys want to come with us this year?" she asked.

"I'll check with Grace, but I'm sure she'd love to go. We don't really have much in the way of family. It'd be good for her to be around someone else's."

"Great. I'll ask Ryan," she said over her shoulder as she headed out of the tent.

Somehow we ended up with no children on the ride home. I'm sure Jillian had something to do with that. We avoided the subject of us and had a pleasant ride home. We stopped at the Archers' to drop off their things and pick up Grace. Once we arrived at our house, Ryan helped us carry in our things.

"Ryan, will you stay and play with me?" Grace asked. "We could play with my new toys."

He looked up at me. Just then, I needed to be alone. I shook my head.

"Sorry, Doll, I've got to get back home. Maybe I'll see you in a couple of days." He looked up at me again. After giving Grace a hug, he stood back up and looked at me. I didn't move, so he said goodbye and left.

Grace settled down to watch a movie, and promptly fell asleep. This left me with a little time on my own to think before dinner. It had begun to rain and storm so I sat out on the porch and tried to relax. I'd been out there for awhile when I realized I missed Ryan. I wanted him here with me, sitting next to me, laughing and talking. I missed him. As I thought about him, a smile came to my face and it lit up my whole attitude. He loved me. He was my best friend, and I did love him. What was I going to do?

I thought about him that night and all day the next day. I couldn't get him out of my mind. That night while we were eating dinner, Grace told me she missed him. That was it, I decided to call him. After I had put Grace to bed, I picked up the phone and dialed his number. But when he picked up the phone and I heard his voice, I couldn't say anything.

"Alyse, is that you?" he asked.

"Yes," I whispered back.

"Are you okay? How's Grace?"

"She's fine. Ryan, would you like to come over?"

"I'd love to."

He was at my door within 15 minutes. I opened the door and fell into his arms. He held me tight and kissed me passionately. Finally, I pulled away and took a deep breath.

"Do you want some dessert?" I asked softly, turning for the kitchen.

He grabbed my wrist. "I want you," he said and pulled me back into his arms.

I pulled away again, trying to catch my breath. "Ryan, I want to talk. I need to talk to you. That's why I called."

He nodded and headed into the kitchen. I stood in the living room trying to catch my breath, and my heart. He came out a few moments later, carrying two bowls of ice cream. He walked past me and headed for the door. "Well, are we going to talk or are you just going to stand there staring at me?" he asked teasingly.

I followed him out onto the front porch, sat next to him on the swing, and took the bowl he handed me. I looked down into the bowl. He had put the fudge topping on in a swirl pattern, just like my father had always done for me when I was a little girl. We ate in silence, watching the quiet street beyond my porch.

Finally he turned to me and took my bowl. "Well," he said.

I looked out over the street again and then turned to face him. I looked into his face and took his hand in mine. "Ryan," I began, and took a deep breath. "I want to give us a chance."

"Oh, Alyse-" he began.

"Ryan, listen," I said as I put my finger up to his lips. "You are a very important part of my life, of Grace's life as well." I paused again. "I want to take this slowly. I need to take this slowly. I am just so unsure of myself, and I –"

This time he put his finger up to my lips. "Anything you say, Alyse," he said huskily. He slid in closer and his lips replaced his finger on my lips. And as he kissed me, I felt it spark something deep inside me, and I prayed it would never burn out.

CHAPTER 14

Over the next few days, Ryan came over every evening. He was also coming with us to the Archers' family Fourth of July celebration. When I called Jillian to find out what time we were leaving, she asked about Ryan. I told her we were seeing each other now, and she told me how happy she was for me.

We left early in the morning of the Fourth. We all rode with the Archers in their van. I was looking forward to a day with Ryan and Grace. The next day, Grace and I were heading north for Drew's wedding.

As soon as we got there, the boys took off. Grace wanted to go with Courtney and I looked to Jillian.

"They'll be fine," she reassured me. "We're out in the country. Alex's family maybe a little weird, but they're good people," she laughed.

Jillian was right about Alex's family. Ryan and I joined in on a few strange games, then listened to Alex's uncle while he told stories of ghost ancestors walking the land at night. They were hilarious. We had a wonderful lunch and a very pleasant afternoon.

"I missed being part of a big family like this," Ryan told me as we walked hand-in-hand around the afternoon festivities.

"Me, too."

Ryan led me over to a swing bench under a shady tree. We sat peacefully watching the children run around and the old people scold them. Suddenly we got hit with a stream of water. We tuned and there stood Aaron Archer with a huge smile on his face. Grace and

Courtney were giggling right behind him. Ryan leaped up and began to chase Aaron. Someone handed him a water gun, and in no time, both of them were soaking wet, but laughing so hard they both fell down. Soon, all three children were piled on Ryan as they tickled each other.

That evening, after a great cookout, we settled back on blankets to watch the fireworks. When they were over, we said our good-byes and were welcomed back again next year. We piled back into the van and headed home.

I leaned against Ryan and went over the day again in my head. Before long, I fell asleep.

The next day, we had breakfast in the city with Ryan before heading north for Drew's wedding. He walked us out to my car afterward. I helped Grace buckle in and then turned to Ryan.

"I'm going to miss you," I said.

"I'm going to miss you, too," he told me.

"We'll only be gone three days. We'll be back on Monday."

"Come here," he said and pulled me close to him. He kissed me deeply as we stood on the busy streets of the city, among strangers who smiled as they passed.

"Are we almost there?" Grace asked.

"Yes, Grace. We are almost to the hotel."

"Does it have a pool?"

"Yes," I told her for the hundredth time. We checked into our hotel half an hour later. I'd left Ryan only that morning and already I missed him so much. I called Drew to let him know we'd arrived while Grace put on her swimsuit. I had her put her clothes back on and we had lunch in the restaurant downstairs. We took a walk around our hotel and then Grace went for her swim. After her swim, I gave her a hot bath and tucked her for a quick nap. After I knew she was sound asleep, I called Ryan.

"Hello." I heard his voice on the other end and could almost feel him near.

"I miss you."

"Alyse, I miss you, too." Just hearing his voice made me feel better. We talked for awhile. Our conversation was about nothing, little things, and yet it was everything.

Grace and I had a quiet evening after another dip in the pool, we ordered room service and played a few games we had brought along.

I lay in bed that night trying to fall asleep. My thoughts kept circling around the same theme - I wanted Ryan here, with me, always.

The next day, Grace and I wandered around Chicago, looking at Museums and exploring. We had lunch then headed back to the hotel to take another dip in the pool, shopping a little on the walk back.

That evening, we had the rehearsal for Drew's wedding. The dinner afterwards was wonderful. Drew's fiancée, Kristin, was just as he had described her, amazing. She seemed to really love my brother and that was what mattered, although she seemed like she had the potential to be a good friend as well. She also thought Grace made the most adorable flower girl and made a fuss over how cute she was in her dress, which made her a hit with Grace.

The morning of Drew's wedding, I was awakened by a phone call. "Hello," I said, expecting to hear Ryan's voice. Instead, Drew's panicked voice answered me.

"Alyse, I'm getting cold feet."

"Drew, calm down. What's wrong?" I asked.

"I don't know."

"You love her, don't you?"

"Yes, more than anything," he responded.

"Then what's the problem?"

"I'm getting married, Alyse. Today!"

"I know," I told him. "She's wonderful, and you love each other, and life together is going to be great, right?"

I heard my brother take a deep breath on the other end of the phone. "I don't know if I am ready for this. I've always been a loner, except with you."

"Drew, take a deep breath, repeat that you love Kristin, and go get married."

"Got it." There was a pause, then, "Thanks, Alyse. I guess I just needed some reassurance."

"You're welcome, big brother. Thanks for the wake up call."

"No problem."

I hung up the phone and looked over at my sleeping daughter. I felt a sense of hope in life. I gently touched her cheek, then headed for the bathroom to take my shower and prepare for my brother's wedding.

"Mommy, where's Uncle Drew?" Grace asked.

"Come on, we'll go find him." I took Grace's hand and set out to find Drew. He found me first.

"Well, here I go."

"You still have an hour," I reminded him.

"How do I look?" he asked nervously, pulling at the cuff of his jacket.

"Great."

"Uncle Drew, do you like my dress?" Grace asked. She twirled around for him.

"Very pretty, Grace. Are you excited?"

She nodded and her eyes lit up. She twirled and danced around. Drew smiled then looked back up at me. "Alyse, thanks for coming up."

"I wouldn't have missed this for the world, Drew. You're getting married. I'm so proud of you. Dad would have been, too."

"You think?" he asked.

I nodded.

"I always thought that you would be the first to get married, Alyse."

"I almost was. Remember?"

"Yeah. Do you regret your decision?"

"No, I don't. I thought I would. At the time it hurt, but it wasn't meant to be. I see that now." I stared off into space for a minute, thinking of Ryan.

"What is it, Alyse?" Drew asked. I turned back toward him. "You just had a huge smile on your face."

"I did?"

He nodded, staring at me intently.

"Remember Ryan Casey?"

"Yeah, he's Devon brother. He's down in Indianapolis, isn't he?" I nodded. My eyes must have given me away. "Alyse, are you in love with Ryan?"

"I don't know. He's my best friend and I do love him."

Drew gave me a hug. "You deserve happiness, Aly."

"Thanks," I told him, giving him a big hug, like the kind we used to share, long ago. It felt good to have our relationship back on the right track. I released him and we smiled at each other, each knowing the other was thinking the same thing. I gave his hand a quick squeeze and then stepped back. "We'd better head back. They're probably wondering what happened to us," I said taking Grace's hand. "Congratulations and good luck."

"Right back at you, little sister."

The wedding was beautiful. I enjoyed the reception afterward. I met all of Drew's friends and Kristin's family. After the bride and groom had had their dance, Drew danced with me. We danced in silence, companionable silence, the kind we had shared many times over the years. I realized we had finally come back around.

"I've missed you," I softly told my brother.

"I've missed you, too. Thank you, Alyse, for everything."

Drew danced with Grace, and I danced with a few others, then we said our good-byes as bride and groom left for their honeymoon. Watching them throughout the evening, I knew my brother had finally made it peace and found happiness. I prayed for the same and yet, I knew in my heart of hearts that I had finally found it as well.

Part Four

Finally Home

Chapter 15

We spent that evening and the next at Drew's apartment, to keep an eye on things and to feed his fish. There was plenty to do in Chicago and I thought Grace and I needed a mini-vacation. But Monday morning, bright and very early, we were on the road heading home. Finally, it was a place I was rushing to get to again.

The ads we shot were going to be released that evening. Ryan was going to bring a pizza to celebrate. When we got home, Grace wanted to play at Courtney's for awhile. I told her that she could, but not for very long, then I walked her down. Jillian and I sat and chatted for awhile. I told her all about my brother's wedding. Then I walked home and unpacked our things. Ryan called a few minutes later.

"Hey, Alyse. I'm leaving right now. I'm going to stop and get the pizza and I'll be there in less than an hour."

"Sounds great. Will you pick up Grace at the Archer's on your way here?" I asked.

"Of course. See you then. I love you," he said.

"See you then, Ryan," I said and then hung up the phone. I'm not sure why I didn't tell him I loved him, too. I still wasn't sure I could return the intensity of what he felt for me. I tried not to let myself ponder it for too long or else I might come up with an answer I didn't like.

Almost an hour later, I heard Grace's laugh as she raced Ryan up to the door. I opened it in time for them to run in. "I win!" Grace exclaimed as she ran to me and gave me a quick hug.

"You're getting too fast, Gracie," Ryan told her. He came over to me and kissed me. I kissed him back, then pulled away and smiled at him, taking the pizza. "Let's eat!" he said, and they followed me into the kitchen.

After we'd eaten, we headed into the living room to wait for my television debut. "While we are waiting, someone needs to get into their pajamas," I said.

"I didn't realize this was a sleepover," Ryan said, a devilish look on his face.

"Not you, Ryan. Mommy means me," Grace told him as she walked by the couch. He reached out and grabbed her, and she squealed as he tickled her.

"Are you sure? Maybe she was talking to me. How do you know?" he kept asking her as he tickled her. She was laughing and trying to answer him at the same time.

"Mommy, help me," Grace managed to get out, although the smile on her face told me she was happy to be trapped. I leaned over and began to tickle Ryan. He let go of Grace enough for her to begin to tickle him too. Then they both started to tickle me. We were one happy tangle on the couch. I laughed so hard my sides hurt. When I could talk again, I asked Grace to go get her pajamas on, again.

"You can come back out to see the ads, but then you need to go to bed." She nodded and then headed off to her room.

"She's a great child, Alyse," Ryan told me.

"Thanks," I said.

"Look, Alyse, I think we need to talk. I-"

Grace ran back into the room and landed on Ryan's lap. He looked down and laughed. "Is it going to come on soon?" she asked.

Ryan nodded and then turned back to me. He mouthed the word 'later', and turned back to the TV. Grace began to squeal when it came on. It was quite short, I was only one small clip, but when it was over, she began to sing, "My mommy's on TV."

"We've created a monster," I told Ryan as Grace jumped off the couch and began to do a little dance.

"Did you like it?" Ryan asked.

"I loved it!" Grace said.

He smiled at her than looked back at me.

"It was weird to see myself on TV, even though it was just a quick shot. Just think of all those people that saw me tonight." If I had only known then, but I just shook my shoulders, stood up and smiled toward my daughter. "Time for bed." She gave Ryan a quick hug than followed me into her room. After she had been read to and tucked in, I came back out. "She was so tired, she fell right asleep," I said, a yawn creeping out at the end.

"I think someone else is tired as well," he replied.

I nodded as I walked toward the door to walk him out to his car. He came up behind me and put his arms around my waist. "We need to talk," he whispered into my ear.

"Can it wait until another time?" I asked, yawning for emphasis.

He let go of me and opened the door. I saw him nod his head very slightly. I walked out ahead of him, feeling miserable for hurting him this way. I was still thinking things through, trying to sort out my thoughts and my feelings. I needed more time. Maybe it was only a buffer, but I still needed it, for just a while longer.

I walked him out to his car. He turned around to face me and leaned back against it. After staring at me for a few moments, he reached out and pulled me close to him and kissed me. He spoke so softly I almost missed what he was saying. "Where are we, Alyse?"

"What do you mean?" I asked, looking out over the quiet street behind him, avoiding his eyes.

"I love you. It's your turn, Alyse. The ball is in your court."

"Ryan, I do love you. You are my best friend. I love being with you, I want to be with you, it's just … I'm not sure that … I've been trying to sort it all out, I've been thinking and … Well …"

I was still avoiding his eyes, so he gently took hold of my face and pulled it down until I had to look him in the eyes. What I found there was everything I needed to clear my mind. My heart was screaming my answer, and this time I knew it with my mind and my soul as well.

I reached out and took his face in my hands. I whispered, "I love you - am in love with you, Ryan." My arms went around him as his went around me and we held each other there, in the moonlight.

"Ryan, I just talked to you twenty minutes ago," I told him. I was trying to hold the phone, spoon out the cookie dough, and keep little fingers out of the bowl. Grace and Courtney just giggled.

"I know, but I just wanted to make sure you aren't a dream."

"I'm not, trust me. I love you."

"I love you, too," he said and we hung up.

The girls and I finished making the cookies and I left them to play while I got ready for dinner. Ryan was taking me out while Jillian watched Grace. I was almost ready when the doorbell rang. "Please answer the door, Grace. Don't open it if it isn't Ryan!" I yelled after her. I heard Ryan's voice as he greeted the girls. "Almost ready," I called out.

"You look gorgeous."

I turned and melted into Ryan's arms. "Thank you. So, where are we going?"

"It's a surprise," he told me. "Ready?"

I nodded. "Let me grab my purse." I picked it up off the bed and followed him into the living room.

"We made cookies today," Grace told Ryan. "Want some?"

"Of course. I'll bet they are delicious." He followed her and Courtney into the kitchen and returned with a package.

"All right, girls, let's get going." We dropped them off at the Archers' and I said a quick hello to Jillian. "Thanks for watching her."

"You're welcome. Have fun tonight."

"I will. Thanks again," I said as I headed back down the walkway to Ryan's car.

It was a wonderful evening with dinner at a French restaurant. It felt like a dream. We got back in the car and Ryan started to take me home. "Oh, wait. I got you something," he said. He searched the entire car, but couldn't find it. "I must have left it at my apartment. Mind if we stop?"

"Sure," I said with false skepticism.

He laughed. "I know what you are thinking, but I really did forget it."

"Sure," I said again, and settled back into my seat.

When we got to Ryan's apartment, I headed for the bathroom, while he looked for the infamous gift. "Found it, right where I left it!" I heard him yell. Then the phone rang. I heard Ryan answer it, and I headed out to the living room. When I got there, he had a strange look on his face.

"Ryan, what-"

He held out his hand for me to stop. I walked up to him and took his hand in mine. I mouthed me first concern – Grace. Thankfully, he shook his head. I felt myself relax a little. I couldn't get anything from his side of the conversation. Then he said, "Hold on," and turned to me. "It's Devon," he whispered. I sucked in my breath. "He saw the commercial on the television. He says he's been trying to get hold of me all night.

"What does he know?" I asked.

"Not much. I've been avoiding his questions."

"Just answer them, Ryan. He'll find out sooner or later anyway." He nodded and brought the phone back up between us, so I could hear.

"I'm back, Devon."

"The company Alyse was modeling for, didn't your ad agency land that account?" When I heard his voice again, I froze as old memories and emotions swept through me. I tightened my grip on Ryan's hand.

"Yes, actually, we did. It was a sizable account."

"Did your team handle it?"

"Yes," Ryan answered simply.

"Then you knew where she was and you didn't tell me?" Devon asked angrily.

"Yes." Ryan voice never wavered.

"How long have you known she was in your area?"

"Devon, why don't you contact her and ask her yourself?"

"Her number is unlisted," was his reply.

"I'm sorry, Devon, but you'll have to contact her yourself. If she wants you to know, she can tell you."

"How am I supposed to get hold of her?" he asked. "Do you have her number?"

"Yes, Devon, but I'll have to ask her if I can give it to you."

"Ryan, I need to talk to her, to hear her voice again. I miss her so much it hurts." He paused, and I could hear him breathe. I dropped Ryan's hand and turned to the window. It had begun to rain and as I watched the raindrops hit the window I felt tears fall from my own eyes. I heard Ryan say, "Hold on," then felt his arms around me. I leaned back.

"I didn't know it would be this hard," I whispered.

"How do you feel?"

I could hear the hidden question. I turned to look in his eyes. "You have nothing to fear. I did love your brother, but I'm in love with you."

He pulled me close and whispered, "I love you," into my ear, his breath hot against my skin. Together, we turned back to the phone.

"I'm sorry, Devon, I can't help you."

"Ryan, I'm begging you. I need to talk to her. If I can only tell her how much I miss her, and how I've wished every night and day that she'd come back to me and tell me it was all a big mistake. I need her, I love her still. Ryan, please … please give me her number."

The tears fell from my eyes and I couldn't hold back as I thought about what I had put him through. "I'm so sorry," I whispered.

"What?" Devon asked.

I was crying so hard that sobs racked my body. I sank down to the ground. Ryan sat down beside me and put his arm around me.

"Ryan? Ryan, are you okay?" Devon asked.

"Yeah, Devon. Hold on."

"Ryan, what's going on?"

"Don't worry about it. I'll call you back later."

"Ryan, wait … Alyse?"

"I'm so sorry," I said again, through my tears.

"Alyse! Alyse, talk to me," Devon said.

"I'll call you back," Ryan told him, and hung up. He pulled me back into his arms and wiped away my tears.

"I'm sorry," I kept repeating.

"Shhh, it's okay. Just relax, take a deep breath."

The phone rang again, but Ryan didn't answer it. He turned the ringer off. I began to relax against him, and let my mind go blank.

I woke up and heard soft breathing next to me. I looked around and began to panic when I couldn't remember where I was. Then I saw Ryan next to me. We were on the floor in his living room. I must have fallen asleep as I leaned against him, trying so hard to forget Devon. He must have fallen asleep, too.

"Ryan," I said, and shook him gently.

"Alyse, what time is it? I must have dozed off. I-I wanted to let you sleep, to relax."

I looked around and found the clock. "It's 1:30. Ryan, I've got to get Grace!"

"Jillian will keep her. I'm sure she's fine. How are you?"

"I don't know. I need to see my daughter."

Ryan stood up and helped me up. My head was pounding, and I leaned on Ryan as he walked me out to his car. I curled up into a ball on the seat and fought back images of Devon waiting for me. As soon as Ryan pulled up in front of the Archers', I flew out and up the steps. The sound of shuffling feet answered my knock.

"Who's 't?" a sleepy voice asked.

"It's me, Alyse," I replied, as Ryan came up behind me.

Jillian opened the door and blinked at the light from the porch. I went right in and found my daughter asleep on the couch. I fell down beside her and pulled her gently into my arms. Tears slipped from my eyes as I watched her peaceful face.

I was oblivious to everything else. Ryan was standing with Jillian, speaking to her in hushed tones. He came over and knelt down next to me.

"Why don't you stay here with Jillian," he said. I shook my head and started to stand up with Grace in my arms. Ryan reached out and helped me up. But when he reached to take Grace, I pulled back.

"I am going home, even if I have to walk," I said quietly and headed for the door. Ryan beat me to it and held it open for me.

"Of course you're not walking," he said as I walked through the doorway. We walked to the car, and he opened that door for me as well. I slid in, with Grace still sound asleep in my arms. Ryan drove us down the street to our house. I got out and he followed me up to the door.

"Thanks, Ryan. I can handle it from here." I had managed to unlocked the door and turned to face him.

"Alyse, I'm not leaving you alone tonight. Let me help you."

"I'm not a child. I can take care of myself!" I tried to make my voice sound forceful, but I was too drained, and I knew Ryan knew it.

He reached out and put a hand on my arm. "You've been through an emotional hailstorm tonight. I don't think you should be alone. Please, let me in."

"I've got Grace," I said and shut the door in his face. I looked down into the face of my sleeping daughter. Gently, I walked back and laid her down on my bed. I changed into my nightgown and lay down beside her. I just watched her for the longest time, while tears ran down my face. Finally, I had to put my face in my hands to try to stifle my sobs. Eventually I just gave up and fell over onto the pillows and cried myself to sleep.

I awoke to soft sunlight playing down onto my face. With my eyes closed I could feel its warmth and was able to breathe deeply. I rolled over and sat up with a start. Ryan was in the chair next to my bed, sound asleep.

"Ryan?" I said softly.

"Shhhh." I turned to find Grace in the doorway with a tray in her hands. "He's asleep."

"Yes, I can see that, sweetheart. But what's he doing here?" I took the tray and found a glass of juice and a bowl of her favorite cereal.

"It's for you, Mommy," she said, a huge smile on her face.

"Thank you, Grace. How did Ryan get here?"

"He was outside," she said, as if that explained it all.

"He was outside our door?"

She nodded. "I heard the paperboy and went to get the paper for you, and-"

"Grace, you know that you are not to go outside or open the door when I'm asleep," I told her sternly.

"I know, but I wanted to surprise you," she said as she presented me with the paper.

"Where was Ryan?" I asked.

"He was asleep on the porch swing. He didn't look very comfortable, so I woke him up. I told him he could have my bed, Mommy, because I was watching cartoons, but- Mommy?"

I set the tray down on the floor and slowly crawled across the bed, staring at Ryan. He still had the same clothes on he'd worn the night before. He'd been worried about me, and he'd stayed. New tears swelled in my eyes and threatened to spill over. But these were not tears of sorrow or guilt, or regret, not anymore – these were tears of joy and of love.

Grace had always been my strength, from the day she was born. She'd kept me going when I'd wanted to quit. I could always look into her face and find what I'd need to push on. I knew why God had saved her, because she in turn had saved me.

Devon had been my comfort when I'd needed it most. He'd been there to see me through my greatest tragedy. But that's all it had been.

But Ryan, he was so much more. He was my passion.

In the back of my brain, I heard Grace as she padded out of the room and shut the door but I could not take my eyes off Ryan. Slowly, I lowered my head and brushed my lips over his. He tipped his head up and his arms came around me, pulling me toward him. As he kissed me, I felt all my doubts, all my fears, melting away as the fire slowly engulfed me, a fire that I knew we would never let burn out.

"I'll get it," Grace yelled as she ran to answer the door.

"Don't forget to ask who it is," I called after her. Ryan come up behind me and put his arms around me, and as I leaned back into them, he began to kiss my neck. "Ryan, you're going to make me burn the eggs," I scolded playfully.

"I don't care," he whispered.

"Then you're going to get very hungry before dinner."

I heard Grace's voice in the living room, along with two others. I held my hand up to Ryan and began to listen.

"-ah-huh, she's in the kitchen with Ryan." I had to strain harder to hear the next line because she'd dropped her voice. "They're gonna get married, then I'll have a daddy."

"Ryan'll be your daddy?" I heard Courtney ask.

"Yep," Grace replied.

"We just came by to see how you were doing," Jillian said, "and to bring you your shoes, Grace."

"Mommy forgot them last night?"

"Yes, it was late and I think she was tired," Jillian explained.

"Ryan was tired, too," Grace said. "He didn't even make it to his car!"

I looked up at Ryan and he was smiling toward the sound of the voices. I took his hand in mine and led him out into the living room. "Hello, Jillian, Courtney." Jillian looked from me to Ryan and smiled. "I hear you've already heard the news."

"Grace was telling us."

Grace ran over to Ryan and he pulled her up into his arms. I smiled up at them and he put his arm over my shoulders. "We're gonna be a real family!" Grace exclaimed.

"Well, we should be going. Come on, Courtney."

"No, stay," Ryan said. "I'll take the girls to the park. Have you had lunch?" he asked them. They both shook their heads, so we all sat down for a quick lunch. As soon as we had eaten, he left with the girls. I made some tea, and Jillian and I sat on the porch swing.

"So, what happened?" Jillian asked.

"He slept out here, all night. I told him I didn't need him and shut the door in his face, but he stayed. Grace let him in this morning, and then he slept in a chair at my bedside." I turned to Jillian. "I love him. He's the part of myself that I've been missing. Now … now I feel whole." I took a deep breath and smiled up at the beautiful, deep blue sky.

"I don't know if I can do this," I told Ryan.

"He will find out sooner or later. He is my brother, you know."

"So I've heard."

"This is the best way, Alyse."

"Yeah, I know. It's just going to be hard," I told him. That was an understatement. My heart was beating wildly and I could barely control the urge to get up and run out Ryan's apartment. I turned and caught Ryan staring at me. His eyes softened.

"It's not going to get easier," he said softly. I nodded and took in a deep breath, then let it out slowly. We sat down on the sofa, each with a phone, while Ryan dialed Devon's number.

"Hello?"

"Hello, Devon. It's me, Ryan."

"What do you want?" Devon snapped.

"I was wondering if you were coming out again for Labor Day weekend?"

"I don't think I can."

"Why not?" Ryan asked.

"I'm busy," was Devon's quick reply.

"No, you're not."

"Do you honestly think you can just call me up, invite me out and make pleasant chit-chat and I'll forgive and forget," Devon said angrily.

"Forgive what, exactly?" Ryan asked patiently.

"Don't play dumb with me, Ryan. You know exactly what."

"Why don't you tell me," Ryan snapped back, losing his patience. I gently put my hand in his, and he visibly relaxed again.

"You stole Alyse from me! You didn't tell me when you knew where she was and kept her for yourself, you son of a-"

"Stop!" I yelled into the phone. "I won't have brothers fight because of me." I looked over at Ryan. "Devon, he didn't tell you … because I wouldn't let him."

"Alyse-" he began.

"Just hear me out. Devon, you are a great guy, and someday you'll find the right woman, but it is not me. You have to let me go," I pleaded. The other end of the line was silent. I heard him sigh. I wanted to cry, but I wouldn't let myself. Enough was enough.

"Devon?" Ryan said.

"I'm here," he said. His voice sounded sad, and I wished I could look into his eyes and reassure him. Instead, I looked to Ryan. His smile was strong, warm. "Why did you call?" Devon said, his voice devoid of any emotion.

"To invite you out for Labor Day weekend," Ryan answered.

"Why does it matter?"

"Devon, you're my brother, and I want you here …"Ryan's voiced trailed of, and he looked over at me. "And I want you to be my best man," Ryan finished quickly.

"What?!" Devon roared.

"Take it easy, Dev-"

"I will not! First I lose her, then you find her, and now you're getting married! And you have the nerve to ask me to be your best man." The line went dead.

"What now?" I asked.

"Why don't you call him, on your own. He'll listen to you. Give him time, and he'll come around."

I nodded. "I'll try."

I wasn't as sure of Devon as Ryan sounded. Ryan was more confident about most things and I trusted his judgment, but I was not thrilled with the prospect. However, I gave him a week to cool off, and then gave it a try. We only had five weeks left until our wedding. So, that night, I read to Grace and tucked her into bed, then headed off into the living room to call Devon, before I could talk myself out of it. My stomach was in knots as I picked up the receiver and dialed his number.

"Hello?" Devon said.

"Hi, Devon," I replied as calmly as I could.

"What do you want, Alyse?" he asked, sounding weary.

"I don't want you to hurt anymore." I heard him laugh, then sigh. "Devon, I didn't plan this. In the beginning, we were only friends. He wanted me to see you, but I wasn't ready, so he kept quiet. He became my best friend. I didn't plan on falling in-"

"Stop! You sure have a funny way of trying to stop the hurt. I don't want to hear any of this."

"Devon, he's your brother. You can't stay mad at us forever. Please, come out here and see us, talk to us, and if you don't want to … if you feel you can't stay," I took a deep breath and finished, "then we'll understand. But, please, at least try."

There was silence on the other end of the line. Finally, he replied, "Alright, for you I'll try."

"Thank you," I replied, but the line had already gone dead.

The next five weeks were very busy as we planned our wedding and headed back to school. It was going to be a small ceremony, just family and close friends. Drew was coming down with his wife. Jillian and Alex would be there, of course, along with a few friends from work and church. The reception would be open to anyone else.

Grace was very excited. She called Ryan "Daddy" once in awhile. She told us she was practicing. Ryan loved it, I could tell by the look on his face. Once we were married we planned to start the process to have Ryan adopt Grace as well.

Finally, the weekend of the wedding arrived. Friday, Drew and Kristin arrived. They were staying in my guest bedroom. That evening, Drew, Kristin, Ryan, Grace and I went out to dinner. Afterward, I put Grace to bed and came back out to the living room.

"She's so excited you guys are here," I told Drew and Kristin. We talked for awhile, then Ryan stood up to leave. I walked him out to his car. When I returned, Kristin was gone.

"She's gone to bed," Drew explained. He looked at me and smiled. "We've come a long way, Aly."

I nodded. "We sure have. So big brother, what do you think of Ryan?"

"I think he'd better be good to you, or he'll have to answer to me." He kept a straight face, but there was a sparkle of laughter in his eyes.

"Honestly, I don't know how your wife puts up with you," I replied, smiling. "Now, seriously."

"Seriously," he began, "I know you two will be happy. I can tell he loves you."

"And I him."

He stood up and gave me a hug. "You deserve this happiness, Alyse."

"Thanks, Drew. Goodnight."

"Goodnight."

The next day, Ryan, Grace and I headed to the airport to pick up Devon. We had a picnic lunch and were planning on meeting my brother and sister-in-law along with the Archers at a park nearby with Devon. I'd been reluctant to bring Grace with us. I wasn't sure how Devon would react to seeing us. But Ryan had said that she was likely to soften the blow, so I'd agreed.

We waited by the baggage claim sign while everyone streamed off the escalators. "Do you see him?" I asked Ryan.

"No, did we miss him?"

"Maybe he didn't get on the plane," I said. I turned to scan the crowd around us again. When I turned back to the gate I saw him and wasn't sure what to do. I wanted to run and give him a hug, but something in his face and the way he was standing froze me to the ground where I stood. Slowly, he came toward us.

"Is that him, Mommy?" Grace asked.

"Yes, Grace," I said. I reached down and picked her up so she could see over the crowd. Devon's eyes widened when he saw her and his pace quickened.

"Is this little Grace?" he asked.

She smiled and I saw his eyes soften. I threw a quick smile at Ryan as we headed to the baggage claim to get Devon's bags. He and Grace chatted; he asked her about kindergarten and what she liked to do. But so far, he hadn't said a word to either Ryan or me. Devon grabbed his luggage and followed us out to Ryan's car.

"We're going to a picnic not far from here. Drew and his wife will be there, along with a few friends," I told him. He only shook his head, a polite gesture to show he'd been listening. It hurt my heart to have him so close and yet so distant. But I understood, this could not be easy for him. The ride to the park was kept alive by Grace's constant flow of chatter.

We quickly parked and made our way toward our party. Drew saw us and began to walk to meet us. "Hey, Devon," he said as he held out his hand. Devon took it warmly. Drew introduced Kristin and the three of them chatted for a moment. I introduced him to the Archers. With the introductions over, we began to set out the food. Devon pitched in and helped us. He was very friendly with the Archers – with everyone but Ryan and me. He wouldn't even look at us. After the picnic, Grace wanted to ride with Drew, and Devon did as well.

"I don't know how much longer I can take this," I told Ryan once we got into the car.

"He'll come around," Ryan said.

"Are you blind? He won't even look at us! How can you possibly say that!"

"He has to, or he'll lose us both. Alyse, we're getting married tomorrow and then Devon will see how much we love each other. He'll realize what was meant to be. He'll come around, he doesn't have a choice. We are all the family he has. And you saw him with Grace, he adores her."

I nodded, but I didn't feel as confident as Ryan did. We got to the house before the others but I couldn't sit still, contemplating how we were going to pass the afternoon until the rehearsal dinner. Would the tension continue? How would I be able to enjoy this special day? I didn't have to wait too long. Drew, Kristin, Devon and Grace all came in smiling and chatting. As soon as Grace saw Ryan, she ran over to him.

"Daddy!" she yelled and squealed when he swung her up into the air and into his arms.

I smiled at them and then turned to the others. The look on Devon's face stopped me in my tracks. His eyes were cold and his face set in stone. I followed his gaze to see he was watching Ryan and Grace. She was giggling as Ryan was tickling her. Turning, I slipped out of the room and walked quickly down the hall to my bedroom and shut the door. I looked back on the years since the accident and felt all my confused emotions, from then until now, race through me. Could I really be happy with Ryan? Could I ever really be happy again?

I took a deep breath and let it out. No more of this, I told myself. I was making the decision to stop doubting myself, to stop second guessing and causing myself so much pain and anguish. From now on, I would step out in confidence and not uncertainty. With my shoulders held high, I stood up and walked back out into the living room. "Grace, will you please go play in your room for a little while." I smiled down at my daughter.

She smiled back at me. "Sure, Mommy." She gave me a hug and skipped out of the room, humming to herself. "Alright, now this has gone far enough," I began and turned to Devon and Ryan. "I want this resolved before my wedding tomorrow. It is going to be a happy day!"

Ryan and Devon both looked at me with surprise. Then slowly they turned and looked at each other. There was a moment of complete silence and then at the exact same time they began to yell at each other. It would have been a very hilarious moment under different circumstances.

Drew and Kristin stood up. They came over to me and gave me a big hug. "Good luck, Alyse," Drew said. "We'll take Grace for an ice cream cone.

"Coward," I told him with as much of a smile as I could muster just then. "But thanks." They must have grabbed Grace and gone out the back because I didn't see them go out, but before long I heard their car. With a sigh, I turned and looked at the two men yelling at each other. "One at a time!" I yelled to be heard above them. They both turned to look at me again. "Alright. No more yelling. We're going to sit here until we get some things sorted out. Nobody leaves here mad. To start with, I'd like to say that each of you is an important part of my life, for different reasons. Devon," I said, taking his hand, "you were there when I needed you most. I'll never forget what you did for me. I'm so sorry I couldn't give you what you wanted, what you needed."

"Why?" he asked gently. "Why couldn't you?'

"You know, I have had a lot of time to think about this – and to think about what I would say if you ever asked me this exact question, which I assumed would never happen." I paused, wanting to get this just right. "Honestly, I didn't know myself. I had to stand my ground and find myself, and I also had to find the strength to do that. I'd been running from everything, trying to hide so nothing would find me. Please understand, it wasn't you."

He closed his eyes and took a deep breath. "What about now?"

"I did love you very much, but I was never in love with you. We'd have been okay, you and me, but you deserve so much more. You deserve the passion and all that comes with it. We both do."

He stared at me for awhile, and it took all my strength to return his gaze, but I did it. I wasn't hiding anymore. Slowly he nodded.

"Do you forgive me, for causing you such great pain?" I asked.

"Of course." He leaned forward and gave me a hug. Slowly, he turned to Ryan.

"Go ahead, say what you feel," Ryan urged.

"It's going to be hard to forgive you, Ryan."

"I understand," he replied. "I'm sorry you were hurt by this, but I want you to know this - I'm in love with Alyse. I would do anything for her. Know that no one could love her as much as I do, and be happy for us, for her."

Devon nodded and held out his hand. Ryan shook and the two brothers embraced.

"Are we going to be okay?" I asked. Ryan smiled and nodded as he slipped his hand into mine.

"It's going to take awhile, and I can't say I'm happy with this," Devon began, "but I wish you both happiness. And if my idiot brother ever does anything stupid, you have my permission to beat him up." And for the first time toward us, Devon smiled.

"Are you ready, Grace?" I asked my daughter. She nodded her head eagerly.

"Ryan's really going to be my daddy now, for really and forever?" she asked.

I nodded, "That's a promise, Grace."

She beamed from ear to ear and began to do a fairy dance around the room.

Jillian laughed and then turned to peek out the door. "It's gorgeous out there," she said. Just then came the signal for Grace to start down the aisle.

"Bye, Mommy. See you when we're a family!" And off she went.

As I waited for my turn, I reflected on my life. And as I did, I found myself facing my future, not with fear but with confidence. It was bright and full of hope and promise. The past began to slide off me like rainwater, I felt it puddle on the floor around my feet. So that's where I left it, behind me, as I started my walk to a new beginning.

CPSIA information can be obtained at www.ICGtesting.com
Printed in the USA
BVOW011625280213

314424BV00002B/237/P

9 781462 718436